The
Seven-Headed Beast
and Other Acadian Tales
from Cape Breton Island

The Seven-Headed Beast *and Other* Acadian Tales *from* Cape Breton Island

Collected by Anselme Chiasson

Translated by Rosie Aucoin Grace

Breton Books
Wreck Cove, Cape Breton Island
1996

Copyright © 1996 by **Breton Books**
Wreck Cove, Cape Breton Island
Nova Scotia B0C 1H0

English-Language Editor: Ronald Caplan
Production Assistance: Bonnie Thompson

The Seven-Headed Beast and Other Acadian Tales from Cape Breton Island is available in French as **Contes de Chéticamp** from Les Editions d'Acadie, Moncton, 1994.

Breton Books gratefully acknowledges translation assistance for this book from the Canada Council.

The Seven-Headed Beast is part of the Large Print Program of the National Library of Canada.

Canadian Cataloguing in Publication Data

Chiasson, Anselme, 1911-

   The seven-headed beast and other Acadian tales from Cape Breton Island

   Translation of: Contes de Chéticamp.

   ISBN 1-895415-42-X

1. Tales — Nova Scotia — Chéticamp.   I. Title.

GR113.5.C43C4413   1996   398.2'09716'91
C96-950049-1

TABLE OF CONTENTS

Publisher's Note

IT IS AN HONOUR to offer this book. I admire these tales for their freshness and boldness, and for the bit closer they draw us to what Andrew Hill Clark called "in many ways, these altogether magnificent people"—the Acadians.

Our thanks to Père Anselme Chiasson for permission to have the tales from his book *Contes de Chéticamp* translated into English.

Our thanks as well to Donald Deschênes for allowing his lovely portrait of Père Anselme in that same book to be translated and included here. Mr. Deschênes also provided the Tale-Types based on Aarne and Thompson's work, a scholarly way of showing that these popular stories are part of the folk literature of the world.

And many thanks to Rosie Aucoin Grace from St. Joseph du Moine, another Acadian community up the road from Père Anselme's Cheticamp, for helping keep these tales alive for an English audience—these passionate, funny, bawdy and tender tales from the heart of Acadian Cape Breton. While we have maintained the order of Père Anselme's book *Contes de Chéticamp*, Ms. Grace has worked not only from the printed tales but from transcripts of Père Anselme's original tapes. If they are a good read, tale by tale, if there are outbursts of laughter and shudders of horror—Ms. Grace has brought us closer to her French Acadian turf.

1

As it happens, Rosie Aucoin Grace is distantly related to the storyteller Marcellin Haché. And Rosie's 100-year-old grandmother Minnie Aucoin was often there when Mr. Haché told tales. Rosie learned this when she went to Minnie for help with Acadian words no longer in common use. Minnie told her that Marcellin was the life of the party. He would mention local people in his stories. He would say, perhaps, "The King had a big garden; and although it wasn't Pat à Joe's garden, it was *still* a beautiful garden"—with Pat à Joe likely right there in the room.

Besides Minnie, Rosie wants to thank others who helped her along the way, including Daniel Aucoin, Augustine Bourgeois, Honora Chiasson, and her father Gerard Aucoin.

Finally, while I am grateful for the trust and assistance many people have brought to this book, responsibility for these texts in English rests, happily, with me.

Ronald Caplan
Wreck Cove
Cape Breton Island
1996

Preface

to *Contes de Chéticamp*

I HAVE KNOWN THE WORK of Anselme Chiasson for more than twenty years, through his *Chansons d'Acadie*[1] and *Chéticamp, histoire et traditions acadiennes*.[2] Personally, I have known him for the last ten years. I have always been captured by the strength and simplicity of his work. It is by his writing and his gestures that Anselme Chiasson communicates his pride in himself and what he is. His writing brings us to the point of re-evaluating who we are and what we have become as a community.

I've always admired his indestructible and unfailing confidence in Acadia, his faith in our future, influencing us to work collectively. There is nothing worse for Anselme Chiasson than a grudge, self-pity and lack of activity. In order to respect ourselves and to be respected, we have to accomplish certain tasks. We have to conquer the fear of others before trying to conquer the world. Life is too precious to vegetate. Anselme Chiasson is a good example of such fervour: always smiling, energetic, generous, enthusiastic, patient and impatient, demanding and conciliating, worrying and confident, daring and timid. These weaknesses as well as his strong points form his strength and vitality. I've known very few men at the age of seventy-nine who would determine to reexamine their life's work and prepare it for publication, and who resume sketching and painting at eighty, who drive their car with the passion of a young man of twenty, who see this period as a rare commodity for self-fulfillment and not as a last resort waiting for death.

Father Anselme is an eminently sympathetic man who is very close to people. No wonder he has become a Capuchin. What is most astonishing about him is the fact that he's filled with wonder at the slightest thing. How often have I seen him arrive, from his height of almost two metres, this species of a giant, his wide smile, sharing with me his discoveries and talking about his many projects, his meetings and his readings.

Contes de Chéticamp [here in English as *The Seven-Headed Beast and Other Acadian Tales from Cape Breton Island*] is a publication made up with the same zest and youth. It's amazing to see him tell about his tales. It is not the serious folklorist or professional that speaks, but instead a child who rediscovers the same stories that persist in his imagination. You seldom see that in an adult. Usually, at forty, these fascinations with kings, castles and thieves such as P'tit Jean are gone, well camouflaged in our childhood. Besides, don't the libraries and editors often classify collections of tales with children's books? Even if our society has civilized Anselme Chiasson, within reason, he always has the sense of wild freedom, perhaps a suête [a powerful southeast wind, typical on the west coast

4

of Cape Breton] that blows next to his ear, always keeping him alert for the next adventure.

In this collection, Anselme Chiasson introduces two remarkable storytellers from his home town, Cheticamp. From Marcellin Haché and Loubie Chiasson we find wonderful stories, such as "The Seven-Headed Beast," "The Princess with Golden Hair" and "The Fountain of Youth"; realistic tales such as "The Mother's Arms" and "The Boy Who Was Good Company"; an animal tale, "The Dog's Remembrance"; and some jokes like "The Little Pig," "The Cow's Urine" and "The Two Fools," manifestations of the wholesome humour of the Chéticantins, the people of Cheticamp.

How very pleasant it was to prepare this presentation of tales as much for the richness of the stories as for the language of the storytellers. I hope you, as the reader, will enjoy it as much as I did. May you be able to rekindle your traditional imagination, that it may warm your soul like a favourite old wool vest!

Donald Deschênes
Centre franco-ontarien de folklore
[Franco-Ontarian Folklore Centre]
Sudbury, Ontario

Introduction

from *Contes de Chéticamp*

CHETICAMP IS AN ACADIAN VILLAGE of 3,500 souls situated on the northwest of Cape Breton Island, Nova Scotia. Facing the Gulf of St. Lawrence, with its magnificent bays and the mountains at its back, this corner of land is one of the most picturesque sites in the Maritime provinces.

It was first colonized in 1782 by Acadians of the Dispersion. Leaving the prisons of England or Halifax after the Treaty of Paris in 1763, they travelled to St. Pierre and Miquelon, Arichat, Prince Edward Island or to Gaspesia, in search of land far away from the English, where they could become peaceful landowners.

The Robins, from Jersey Island in the English Channel, had already established a fishing harbour at The Point in Cheticamp by 1767. Their presence assured the pioneers an easy market for their fish and a source of supplies for the products they could not raise or make themselves.

Because of the lack of accessible roads, the people of Cheticamp remained for a long time isolated as if they were on an island. The ocean was their only communication link for a century, thanks to their sailboats, and then to the services of a steamboat until the 1930's.

In the past, the people of Cheticamp cultivated their land, raised livestock and produced the vegetables that they needed. They also participated in the fishing trade in order to make money to buy things through the local merchants, to pay their taxes to the state and their tithe to the church.

Since the creation of the Cape Breton Highlands National Park at its door and the abundance of tourists that come, Cheticamp was able to construct roads that lead to different parts of the village and that, with the automobile, opened doors to the outside world.

This new reality has changed the economy of Cheticamp since the 1930's. The cultivating of the land and the raising of livestock were practically abandoned, while the fishing and tourist trade developed and expanded. Today, this locality is world renowned for its hooked rugs.

Cheticamp has become a modern village, with a magnificent church, a regional school, a hospital and businesses. Doctors, lawyers, tradesmen, and salesmen are equally part of the community. Services such as newspapers, radio, television, entertainment clubs and organized sports also exist. Formerly, none of that existed and people created their own forms of entertainment. Playing ball in the fields during the summer, skating on the lakes and bays during the winter were basically the only sports they played then. However, the cultural and social aspect of their lives was perhaps more intense in those days than it is now. It was certainly different. Card games, songs, stories and occasionally house dances enlivened Sunday afternoons and the evenings.

In Cheticamp, the repertoire of songs and stories seemed to be inexhaustible. More than five hundred songs have already been published, texts and melodies, in eleven collections entitled *Chansons d'Acadie*.

A large number of these are still known and sung.

As far as stories, their number is equally impressive; the number of the storytellers, too. Cheticamp knew its celebrated storytellers, such as Petit Paul LeBlanc, La Grande Souquie, John Marteau, Petit Paddé Roach, Charles (à Lagode) Bourgeois, Jean (à Cécime) Deveau, William (à Jules) Deveau, Marcellin (à Cyrille) Haché, Loubie L. Chiasson and others.

For special occasions, the services of a storyteller were called upon for entertainment, much as those of a fiddle player for weddings. Someone would go get him by wagon and at the end of the evening drive him back home, often slipping him a little tip.

"The storyteller, sometimes completely illiterate, was an artist. He knew how to bring his characters to life for his audience. We often remember Petit Paddé who would start his stories sitting down, but soon got so wrapped up in the heat of the narrative, he'd be standing up and making all the necessary gestures to tell his story."[1]

What was the source of these stories from

Cheticamp? Many were certainly brought over from France by our ancestors and transmitted from one generation of storytellers to another; some were learned from Canadian storytellers in the workplace [from *chantiers*: timber yards, coal yards, shipyards, building yards, lumber camps]; others were heard in seaports from Canadian and French sailors. Finally, some were perhaps drawn from storybooks or almanacs.

Unfortunately, few of these stories have survived. Of the hundreds that seem to have existed in the old repertoire, Gérald E. Aucoin collected a dozen and I collected seventeen; three others were collected by different people. It looks like that's all.

In a beautiful book titled *L'oiseau de la vérité*,[2] Gérald E. Aucoin published nine stories from Jean Z. Deveau and three from Marcellin Haché. We are publishing here twenty stories from Marcellin Haché and three from Loubie Chiasson.

Our storytellers, Marcellin Haché and Loubie Chiasson, had only grade five or six education. They knew and still used the archaic language from the seventeenth century. Their stories, to which we have tried to stay faithful, vividly illustrate the language that our Acadian pioneers brought from France. It would have been simple to transpose these stories to modern French, but it would have removed much of the spontaneity and richness from these stories which, incidentally, are easy to read....

Mrs. Nancy Schmitz, professor of Anthropology at Laval University, identified our stories with the help of *The Types of the Folklore* by Antti Aarne and Stith Thompson. At the time, she worked at the Centre d'études acadiennes at the Université de Moncton.

We want to thank Carole Saulnier, co-ordinator of the management program of the Archives de folklore of the Université Laval, who authorized us to publish the tale "The Beautiful Helen," collected from Marcellin Haché in 1960 by the late Luc Lacourcière.[3]

We also want to thank Robert Richard from the Centre d'études acadiennes of the Université de Moncton for his support, his research and for all the records and manuscripts provided to us.

We would like to express our sincere gratitude towards Donald Deschênes, director of the Centre franco-ontarien de folklore in Sudbury, Ontario, first for his valuable advice, then for his too laudatory preface, finally for his scientific presentation and analysis of every tale contained in this volume. Let's add a special thanks to Mr. Jean-Pierre Pichette, director of the Folklore Department of the University of Sudbury, who supervised all the work toward *Contes de Chéticamp*.

Father Anselme Chiasson
Capuchin

Mr. & Mrs. Marcellin Haché

Tales from Marcellin Haché

THERE USED TO BE quite a few storytellers in Cheticamp. They had become scarce by 1957 when I tried to collect tales. The only traditional storytellers still living at the time seemed to be Marcellin (à Cyrille) Haché and Loubie Chiasson.

Marcellin Haché was born in Cheticamp on November 6th, 1879. He attended school up to grade four or five. He was already fishing with his father at the age of fourteen. After having worked as a lumberjack in Cape Breton, he went to Halifax to learn the carpentry trade. He moved back to Cheticamp, where he married Anne LeBlanc in 1901 and they had ten children. He died on May 22nd, 1974, at the age of ninety-four.

He had learned his tales by hearing them told by other storytellers, first in Cheticamp and then out on work sites. Apparently he had a very good memory.

In this book, we're publishing sixteen of Marcellin's tales and four of his jokes. I collected all of them except "The Beautiful Helen," which was collected by Luc Lacourière in 1960, and the two jokes "The Cow's Urine" and "The Lovers," of which we are presenting only a summary as we were unable to locate their original collectors to obtain permission to publish a complete version.

Mr. Haché was seventy-eight years old in 1957 when I recorded his tales on tape. He was still a great talker and told his stories with much warmth and enthusiasm.

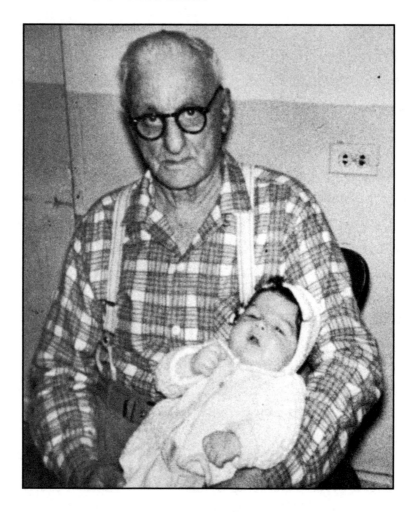

1. The Black Dog
Le Chien noir

This tale[1] belongs to Type 708,[2] *The Wonder-Child*. A poor girl gets married to the King's son and a spell is cast upon her by a rival: she will give birth to a black dog (Ia). She gives birth to a black dog after having withdrawn to sea to deliver (IIb). She discovers that it's a talking dog. This dog goes to the castle to attain help for his mother. The King and the Queen are surprised to find out that the dog's mother is not a bitch but their daughter-in-law (IIIa). One day, the dog saves a young girl who is caught by thieves. He proposes to her as a reward (IIIa). Her father agrees to give his daughter's hand in marriage to a dog—which delivers him from the spell (IVb).

This tale has been found in various Scandinavian and Eastern countries, in Europe and as far away as Australia.[3] There are more than twenty versions in French America.[4] This version was the only one recorded in Nova Scotia.

The Black Dog

THE STORY OF THE BLACK DOG is about a King's son who had two girl friends. There was one who was rich but she was ugly, and the poor one was very beautiful. One day, he decided which girl he wanted to marry. He decided to marry the poor one because she was so beautiful. The rich girl—it didn't suit her at all, she was not very happy about this.

One day, the two girls met on the street. "Ah," said the rich girl, "you're going to marry the King's son and I'm going to be left behind."

"Well," the poor girl replied, "it's not my fault. He asked me to marry him and I'm going to marry him."

"Marry him and I guarantee you that if you have any children, it will not be a child but instead a black dog."

Good! All right.

When the time came, ah! my friend!—she saw that something was coming, something wasn't right.

She said to her husband, "I think I'm going to hire a yacht and have my delivery at sea."

"Oh," he said, "as you wish. I have lots of money."

He hired a doctor and nurse for her and she went on the yacht, she went to sea. Well, not long afterwards she delivered—and instead of a child it was a black dog. The doctor asked her what he should do about this.

She replied, "Does he want to live?"

"Yes."

She said to the nurse, "Well, care for him and let him live."

When the dog was one year old, the dog was big, like this. [The storyteller indicates a metre in size.] He was sitting right next to his mother. She said, "If only you could talk."

"Ah!" the dog said, "I do talk. If you had asked me earlier, I would have talked."

"Well," she said, "if you can talk, you're going to be useful to me." She then said to the captain, "We're going to go back to our country, but you will anchor the yacht behind an island in the harbour away from the view of the King's castle."

He docked the yacht there and she said to her dog, "You're going to go on land. You will go to the King's castle where they will be having dinner. Bring me the best piece of meat that's on their table."

The dog dove into the water, swam to shore, then ran to the King's castle. The door was open and he went and took the piece of meat—but the King's son didn't know what this meant. The dog returned to the boat.

The next day she said to the dog, "You will go to the King's castle and tell the King's son to prepare his best horse and buggy to come and get me."

Well, the King, Queen and son thought that he was only a dog but since he asked them to get his mother, the King said, "Take the old horse and buggy."

The dog replied, "No, I want you to take the best horse and buggy to pick up my mother."

Well, the King's son eventually had to give in. When he got near the shore with his horse and buggy, he saw two officers coming from the boat with a woman. When she got closer, he recognized his wife. They embraced and left together with the dog by their side. When they arrived at the castle, the King and Queen expected to see their son and the dog's mother. They recognized their son's wife and went to her, hugging her and very happy to see her. They were very excited!

Well, the son built a house for himself and his wife, and the King and Queen lived in the old house. One evening, after about a year, their dog told the King's son—he never called him his father but instead "the King's son." The dog said to the King's son, "Tonight we'll go visit that house over there, where you see the light. We have to go there."

The King's son's wife signalled for him not to say no, to say yes. So he said, "Well, we're going to go."

They left and when they had gone a little ways, they heard a woman's cry. It sounded like a girl in trouble. The dog said to the King's son, "You see the house where there's a light, you go there. I'm going to run and see what's making the girl scream like that."

When he got there, two thieves had stolen the girl. He chased off the thieves. He said to the girl, "I'm here to save your life."

"Well," she said, "I cannot return home alone, I don't know where I am."

He said, "I'll lead you home."

He led the girl, and when they arrived at her home, she said, "Now I'm home."

He asked the girl, "What are you going to give me for saving your life?"

"Well," she said, "whatever you ask for, I will give it to you."

He said, "After a year and a day, if I come to you for your hand in marriage, will you marry me?"

"Yes."

All right. He bid her good-bye and he left. He then went where his father was, where the King's son was. He went there. When it came time to leave, they went home.

After a year and a day, the dog told the King's son (he still didn't call him his father), "We're going to go visit where I had saved that girl."

They went there. They entered, the King's son and his dog. The dog spoke and said to the man of the house, "I am here to ask your daughter's hand in marriage."

"What!" he replied. "Give away my daughter in marriage to a dog? That is impossible!"

The girl was in her room. She heard and she came out. She looked at the dog and recognized him. She said, "Papa, this is the dog that saved my life from those thieves, and for his reward he asked for my hand in marriage after a year and a day, and I gave my promise."

"Well, if you promised," he said, "then marry him."

So it was done. She said yes. The dog then said to the King's son, "You stay here and I'm going to go outside and I'll be back in five minutes."

After five minutes, he came back: the most handsome young man they'd ever seen. He went to his father and said, "Shake my hand, Papa, you are my father. I was turned into a dog by a girl who had cast a spell on my mother, and to break the spell I had to find a girl who would marry me while I was a dog. Now the spell is broken and I am a man like any other, and never will I be a dog again."

That's all.

2. The Fountain of Youth

L'Eau qui rajeunezit

This tale from Marcellin Haché[1] corresponds to Type 551, *The Sons on a Quest for a Wonderful Remedy for their Father.*[2] It borrows from Type 676 the magic formula *Open Sesame*. It shares its last three incidents with the Tale-Type 304: *The Hunter*.

This tale is very widely distributed across the world. It's found in the following countries: Finland, Sweden, Russia, England, France, Belgium, Italy, the two Americas, even Africa and India.[3] Paul Delarue and Marie-Louise Tenèze made a list of thirty-seven versions in French Canada, of which three come from Nova Scotia.[4]

The Fountain of Youth

THE FOUNTAIN OF YOUTH is a story about a king who had three sons. The youngest of the three was the wisest but very much frowned upon by his brothers. When he tried to do something, they stopped him; when he went to speak, they stopped him—and he could never get a word in any conversation.

But one day the King was reading his newspaper when he found an article which described a Fountain of Youth that really existed in the world, but it did not say where this water could be located. The King said to his two eldest sons, "I will give you a sufficient amount of money for your voyage from place to place, from country to country, and maybe someone will tell you where this Fountain of Youth might be."

"Ah, yes, Papa," the sons said. "But what will you do with our youngest brother who's always in the way?"

"Ah!" the King replied, "I'm going to chase him away."

They then proceeded to take the youngest son, covering his mouth with a handkerchief so nobody would hear him scream, and put him nearly two hundred feet into the forest, leaving him there.

Although he was the King's son, he found himself poor and with nothing to eat. His brothers had left with their frigate and lots of money, on their way to search for the Fountain of Youth. They travelled from place to place, speaking to people who knew of the Fountain of Youth, but nobody knew where it was.

Meanwhile, the youngest son had spent the night under a tree. When he woke up the next morning, a woman appeared in front of him while he was saying his prayers. She asked, "Do you know me?"

He replied, "No, I've never seen you before."

"No," she said, "you've never seen me before, but I'm your godmother who died when you were still a baby in the cradle." She explained: "Your two brothers went out to try and find the Fountain of Youth but they will never find it. I will tell you how to find this water that can make your father young again. Do you know how to write?"

"Yes."

"Do you have a piece of paper and a pencil?"

"Yes."

"Well," she said, "write down everything I say. The Fountain of Youth is situated in a big black mountain in China, in an underground tunnel. Ask your father to give you his smallest frigate and five hundred dollars in silver, then go into China, put your boat in the harbour. You will see a beautiful road which goes up a big black mountain. When you get there, you'll find a steel door, all cemented in. Even if you hired a thousand men, they wouldn't be able to open the door. The door will open if you say the following words: 'Open Sesame'—the door will open; 'Close Sesame'—the door will close."

The youngest son wrote down what she said. He obeyed what his godmother had told him to do, approached his father and asked for his smallest frigate and five hundred dollars. His father said, "Are you crazy? I'm going to get rid of you anyway."

The youngest son left. He followed his godmother's instructions, and when he came to the steel door he said, "Open Sesame"—the door opened. "Close Sesame"—the door closed behind him. He then went down a stairway. Every twenty feet, there was a small light going down the stairs.

When he reached the bottom, he discovered a beautiful castle, a thousand times better than his father's. He had never seen anything like it.

He could hear his godmother's words: "Go to the fourth door to the left, you'll enter a room, there's a barrel with a leaky tap. Don't touch the tap. Put your bottle under the tap and let it fill up on its own. You can then go through the entire castle without any harm coming to you."

Sure enough, he put the bottle under the dripping tap and went on to explore the castle. All of a sudden, he opened a door which led to a room where the most beautiful girl lay in a bed. He went to her and saw that she was sleeping. He shouted—not a word. He shouted again—nothing. He shook her—nothing. She didn't wake up. He tried everything he could to wake her, but to no avail. He said to the sleeping girl, "You don't want to wake up. Well, I'm going to sleep with you anyway."

He slept with the girl. But when he believed it was time to go, he retrieved his bottle and went back up the staircase. "Open Sesame"—the door opened. "Close Sesame"—the door closed.

He then went off to find his boat and told his captain, "We are going to leave for home."

When they had gone quite a ways, everything was calm. He took his binoculars and looked towards the shore. He saw a battle. People were fighting among themselves. He said to the captain, "I'm going to anchor our ship. Put a boat down. I'm going to see what this battle is all about."

24

When he got to the shore, he saw that it was his two brothers who were involved in the fight. He approached a man and asked, "Why is there a dispute going on here?"

"Well," the man replied, "do you see those two guys?"

"Yes."

"Well," he said, "they've been boarding at the hotel. They came here on their father's boat, sold it for next to nothing so that they'd have money to drink. They've spent all their money. Now they're trying to escape from paying a debt of two hundred dollars they owe the hotel manager."

The youngest son asked, "If I was to pay their debt, could I have those two guys?"

"Ah!" he said, "for sure."

The man showed him the way to the hotel manager. The youngest son said, "Release those two guys and I'll pay their debt."

"Ah!" he said, "yes. I'll give them to you right away."

He gave the hotel manager the two hundred dollars and brought the two brothers with him which was certainly a mistake on his part. He told them about the Fountain of Youth which he had found for their father. They ended up stealing from him. It was while the youngest son was sleeping in his room.

The two brothers figured it wouldn't do that their brother was going to inherit half of their father's fortune. (The King had already told them

25

that if they brought back water from the Fountain of Youth, they would receive half of his fortune and his crown.) The others would receive nothing.

They started searching through their brother's room and found the bottle of water under his pillow. It was the same colour as salt water. They exchanged the water in the bottle—the water that came from the Fountain of Youth—with salt water, and put it back under the pillow. Not a word.

When they all got back to the King's castle, the youngest son announced, "My two brothers, Papa, went in search of the Fountain of Youth but couldn't find it. I found that water myself."

"Yes?"

"But," he said, "you have to follow the directions. For example, you should drink a full glass of the water without stopping."

The King filled up a glass of water and exclaimed, "Oh, it's like salt water." He drank it all and became violently sick to his stomach. He threw up. My dear, he nearly threw up his heart. The older brothers were watching and said, "It is us who found the real Fountain of Youth, not him."

The youngest brother was about to defend himself, to say that they had stolen it, when once again he was taken, mouth covered, and put in the forest where he had been left before. The brothers gave their father the real water and the King became twenty-five again, physically and mentally—as smart as a man of twenty-five. Every day after this, the King would say, "If I had my hands on my youngest son, I'd beat him for making me drink that salt water."

This went on for a year and a day. After a year and a day, the largest warship they'd ever seen entered the harbour. An officer was sent to seek out the King and bring him aboard the ship. The King went on board and was approached by a woman. She said, "You have found the Fountain of Youth, Mister King?"

"Not me, but my eldest son."

"Find him and send him to me."

The King returned home and spoke with his son. "There's a woman on board the ship who wants to see you."

The woman had not revealed to the King what she wanted from his son. When the eldest son went to the ship, the woman asked him, "Was it you who found the Fountain of Youth for your father?"

He replied, "Yes."

"Where did you find it?"

The eldest son made up a story because he didn't know where it was from.

"It was not you who found the water. Tell your father if I don't have the man who found the Fountain of Youth within one hour, I'll call my army and destroy this entire city in a matter of ten minutes."

The eldest son went to his second brother and said, "It's you she wants to see."

The second eldest son went on board the ship. He did like the first one; he also made up a story about where he had found the water.

The woman said, "It's not you either. Tell your father that he has half an hour to come up with the man who really found the water, or I shall destroy this city."

The King confronted his sons and said, "So, you stole the water of the Fountain of Youth from your youngest brother. It was he who actually found it."

"Yes."

"Well, where is he?"

Ah well, they didn't know. Meanwhile, the youngest of the sons, after having heard a cannon shot from the ship, had come to the shore. When his family left the castle to search for him, they found him and told him, "Hurry, go aboard the ship."

The young man went aboard the ship.

The woman asked, "Was it you who found the Fountain of Youth for your father?"

"Yes."

"Where did you find it?"

"Well," he said, "I found it in a big black mountain in China!"

She said, "How did you open the door?"

"Well," he said, "I said some words."

She told him to go ahead and say the words.

He said, "'Open Sesame'—the door opened, and 'Close Sesame,' and the door closed."

The woman tapped him on the shoulder and said, "It is you who found the Fountain of Youth. Come with me."

She guided him into a bedroom, only to find

the most beautiful little girl. The girl had been born as a result of the night he'd slept with this woman.

The woman said, "I was under a spell in that castle. I was to die while sleeping unless I could give birth to a child. Now I have delivered a child like any other woman, and you are my man."

The King came to see his youngest son, got down on his knees and begged for forgiveness for all the suffering he'd caused him. He also offered him his crown and half his fortune.

The woman said, "No. Mister King, you are mistaken. I believe I'm as rich as you are. All I wanted was your son."

They waved good-bye and left.

As for me, I have written two letters, but she never answered.

3. The Little Pig
Le Petit Cochon

In French Canada this joking tale,[1] which has for a theme *The Wager that Sheep are Hogs*, Tale-Type 1551, and in this version, *Un cochon qui serait lièvre*, is most often completed by Tale-Type 1538, *The Youth Cheated in Selling Oxen*.[2] Here, a young man leaves with five dollars in his pocket to buy a pig. On his way back, three thieves dupe him and take his pig. After a while, through his slyness, he manages to punish the thieves and recovers his possessions with good interest.

This tale is found in Spain, Germany, Italy and in North and South America.[3] Of the twenty-one Canadian versions,[4] four are Acadian.[5]

The Little Pig

THE STORY OF THE LITTLE PIG. There was a widow who had a farm, and she kept a cow.

One day her son said, "Mother, we could surely keep a pig—there's many leftovers that go to waste."

His mother replied, "Yes, but how are you going to go get a pig?"

"Well, just give me five dollars," he said. "I will go to the city and buy a pig."

His mother said, "Yes, but you have to go through the country of the thieves. They most certainly will steal your pig."

"Ah! no," he said.

Anyway, she gave him the five dollars. He went to the city and purchased a pig. On his way home, three thieves saw him coming. One of them said to the other two, "One of you will go hide further down, the other hide here, and I will go meet him. I'm going to say to him, 'That's a rabbit you have there, not a pig.' He's going to deny this and say no. I'll then say to him, 'The first man who comes along, if he says it's a rabbit will you give it to me?'"

"Ah! yes!"

The boy with the pig didn't know about this plan. He soon met up with one of the thieves. The thief said to him, "You had a rabbit in one of your snares this morning? Me, I didn't have any."

The boy replied, "It's not a rabbit. It's a pig I paid five dollars for in town."

The thief said, "Well, they sure cheated you. You can get a rabbit for twenty-five cents and you paid five dollars for it. The first man that we meet along the way, if he says this is a rabbit, will you give it to me?"

He answered, "Yes, I will give it to you."

They met up with the next man, who said, "You had a rabbit in your snares. I didn't have any."

The widow's son said, "You're all crazy, I'm telling you it's a pig that I paid five dollars for in town."

"Well," the thieves said, "we are telling you

31

that it's a rabbit. They played a trick on you, selling a rabbit to you for five dollars. If we meet another man who says the same thing, that it's a rabbit, will you give it to us?"

He said, "Yes, I will give it to you."

They met the third thief and the same story went on: "You were lucky to catch a rabbit in your snares. I didn't have any."

Then he realized that they were thieves, but he didn't show it. He gave his pig to them.

When he returned home, his mother asked, "What's new?"

"Well," he said, "Mama, it happened just like you said, the thieves stole my pig. That was a waste of five dollars."

"Well," his mother said, "I told you."

After fifteen days, he said to his mother, "I have to get paid for that pig one way or another. You'll come with me. We're going to go over to the thieves' house. I'm going to dress up as a girl, paint my face and disguise myself with a nice figure and you'll ask if we can sleep there."

"Ah!" his mother said, "okay."

They took off to ask the thieves if they could sleep there. The thief answered, "Yes, but if you want to sleep here, I have to sleep with your daughter."

"Ah! well," she said, "that's none of my affair." The son disguised as her daughter said, "Yes."

They put some bedding for the old woman by the door, and the thief took the daughter upstairs.

A thief sleeps stark naked. So this one went to bed stark naked. The girl (the son of the widow he thought was a girl) said to him in a girl's voice, "I don't sleep with the lamp on." The thief replied, "Well, blow it out, it doesn't bother me."

After the lamp was out, the son of the widow had hidden a stick of hard wood under his robe. He beat up the thief, breaking his ribs in three places. He said to the thief, "I'm not a girl. I'm the widow's son that you stole a pig from, and you have to pay me for it."

The thief asked, "How much do you want?"

"Well," he said, "I want one hundred dollars for all the trouble you caused me."

He had no choice but to give him the one hundred dollars. Then the widow's son and his mother returned home.

At nine o'clock the next morning, the thieves were up and wondering why the other thief was still upstairs with the girl. They went upstairs and opened the door to the bedroom only to find their brother beaten half to death, with three broken ribs.

"What happened to you?"

The thief answered, "That was not a girl that was here last night, it was the widow's son. You're going to have to get a doctor or I will die."

The widow's son figured they would go for the doctor, so he disguised himself as the local doctor. He put on a little beard, bought himself a bag, and made his face just like the doctor's. Then he went walking on the doctor's road. The thieves believed this was the doctor. They asked him, "Could you take care of our master—or he will die."

He replied, "Well, I was leaving for the city but I'll drop by."

He went over to the house and asked the thief, "What did you catch?"

The thief replied, "Well, I'm getting these pains in my side."

He then said to the thief, "Ah! Don't tell me lies. I'm a doctor and I know that these are bruises."

He had given these bruises to the thief himself but the thief thought he was the doctor.

He said to the thief, "Well, there's not much I can do. If I had two different barks, bark from white maple and white birch trees, with the stuff in my bag, I could come up with a cure. I guarantee you that in three weeks, you'd be cured. I just don't know where to find this."

"Ah!" the other thieves said, "we know where to find this."

The thieves left, each with a bag over his shoulder, in search of bark from white maple and birch trees. While those thieves were gone, the widow's son disguised as the doctor took out his stick of hard wood and beat up the thief again. He said to the thief, "Just to let you know that I'm not the doctor but instead the widow's son that you stole a pig from, and you have to pay me for it again."

The thief gave him fifty dollars which came to

one hundred and fifty dollars for the pig. The widow's son then said, "By noon tomorrow, if I don't have my pig back in its pen, I'm going to come here and kill all three of you."

When the other two thieves got back, they asked their brother, "Where is the doctor?"

"Ah!" he said, "it's not the doctor that you brought here, it was the widow's son again." Then he said, "I had to give him fifty dollars more, and he said that by noon tomorrow, if we didn't have his pig in its pen, he'd come here and kill all three of us."

They replied, "Well, let's take the pig back right away!"

There was a snowstorm that day. They hitched the horse to a sled and put the pig on the sled. When they arrived at the farm, the thieves asked where they should put the pig. The widow's son spoke harshly to them to scare them and said, "Well, put him in his pen. You know that a pig doesn't go in the house, it belongs in a pen."

They put the pig in its pen and started to get their horse ready to return home when the widow's son said, "Don't go home, it's too stormy. Put the horse in the barn and come to the house."

They went to the house. The widow's son asked, "Did you have supper yet?"

They replied, "No."

He then asked them, "What would you like for supper, maybe some porridge?"

Even if they hadn't liked porridge, they were

too scared to say anything. They were very afraid. The widow's son put a big pot on the stove and poured in a whole bucket of rolled oats. One of the thieves said to the other, "If we have to eat all that, we're in big trouble."

Anyway, when the porridge was ready, they each filled a lovely big bowl. The first bowl was all right. But then the widow's son said, "You'll eat some more, won't you?"

"Well," they answered, "yes."

All right. After they finished their second bowl, he said to the thieves, "You'll have some more. You have to eat it all because I made it just for you."

Again they had to fill their lovely big bowls for the third time. They were stuffed so full. They had to push their spoons to their mouths with their hands in order to swallow, really force themselves to eat.

When it was time to go to bed, he asked the thieves, "Well, I guess you'd like to go to bed now?"

They answered, "Yes."

He then said to the thieves, "See here, my two boys. You ate so much porridge you are liable to soil your bed. But my good fellows, if you soil the bed, I'll have your lives in the morning.

He put them on the second story, upstairs. They were to sleep in one bed. A thief always sleeps stark naked. They laid down face to face and fell asleep. When they were in a deep sleep, the widow's son took some porridge that was left over in the pot and filled up two plates. He carefully lifted the blankets and placed a plateful of porridge right at their bum. This didn't wake them. The widow's son returned downstairs and stood at the foot of the stairs.

All of a sudden, one of the thieves woke up. He went to move around and felt with his hand. It was.... "Ah! God," he said to the other. He then said, "Get up, I've soiled the bed." The other thief woke up and also felt with his hand and said, "Me, too."

The widow's son then said, "What do I hear, that you have made a mess in the bed? I'm going to come up there and beat you up."

The thieves jumped up, grabbed their clothes in their arms, opened the window and threw themselves to the ground, and ran home!

The widow's son had now inherited a horse and sled that the thieves had forgotten, plus one hundred and fifty dollars for his pig. The thieves had fed the pig, he was now a nice big pig. They had the pig slaughtered. It weighed thirteen pounds.

So that's all there is for the pig!

4. The Mother's Arms

La Femme
aux bras coupés

This wonderful tale[1] is a supernatural story belonging to Type 706: *The Maiden Without Hands*. It consists of a young girl whose brother has to cut off her hands in order to punish her for all the grave mistakes she's done, which was all a ploy made up by her slanderous sister-in-law.

A King's son marries the young girl in spite of her mutilations. Because of her mother-in-law's slander and interference, the girl and her two children are put into exile. It is by a miracle that she recovers her hands and is reunited with her husband.

This cruel tale has been the source of much interest since the Grimm brothers.[2] To this day, more than a dozen studies have been dedicated to this story.[3] It brings to mind certain important themes of medieval literature in which "the heroines of tales and novels are usually accused of having eaten or killed their children or of having given birth to animals. Helpless towards this injustice and cruelty, these women let themselves be tortured and exiled. These stories were created in a society where such primitive cultures and traditions existed."[4]

This tale appears in France in the written literature as early as 1270 and has been abundantly exploited since.[5] Let's go back, for example, to the hymn "L'Histoire admirable de sainte Geneviève de Brabant," published in the *Cantiques de Marseille*.

When Hélène Bernier studied this hymn in 1971, she found thirty-five versions in North America, of which twelve were from Acadia and two in the Indian languages.[6] Father Anselme Chiasson collected another version of this tale in 1957—*La Belle Hélène*—from Mr. Charles Bourgeois of Cheticamp.[7] Luc Lacourcière recorded this same tale, *La Belle Hélène*, from Mr. Marcellin Haché in August 1960.[8]

The Mother's Arms

THERE WAS A WIDOW who had a son and a daughter, and one morning the boy said to his mother, "I'm leaving to go make a living with my gun."

"Well," the daughter said, "if he's going, I'm going too."

They walked all day without finding anything. That night, on the side of the road, they found a log cabin. They went in the cabin. The boy said to his sister, "We'll stay here for the night. There are two beds. We'll sleep one in each bed."

The next morning, he said to his sister, "You're going to stay here and cook. You'll make dinner and I'll go see if I can kill something, maybe some rabbits or partridges."

All of a sudden, he found a fence, a nice big field, a beautiful big farm, a beautiful big house. He went over to the house. The man of the house asked,

"What are you looking for here with your gun?"

The boy answered, "Oh, I'm looking for work here and there."

The man of the house replied, "I would take a man to work on my farm."

"Yes? But," he said, "I can't. My sister is in the cabin over there in the forest and I can't leave her there all alone."

The man replied, "Oh, but you can't stay there. That is a cabin that I built for trappers in the fall. I hire two men who go set traps and snares for pelts, so she can't stay there. Well, just get your sister and I'll hire her too."

The man of the house—his wife had died, leaving him with a little baby and another girl who looked after his child. After getting his sister from the woods, the boy brought her to the farm, and the man of the house said, "You will look after the baby and my daughter will do the housework. Take care of the baby."

The boy was to work on the farm with the man.

Every morning, the boy would hug his sister before going to work. Suddenly, he fell in love with the farmer's daughter. He married the farmer's daughter. But he continued to do the same thing every morning—hugging his sister before going to work. The wife became very jealous because her husband would hug his sister. She asked her husband, "Why do you do that?"

"Well," he said, "it's a promise I made to my

mother, that every morning before leaving for work, I would hug my sister. I have to do it."

He had three lovely horses. The farmer had signed everything that he owned over to him. No money, but he had signed over the farm and the house, everything. He had kept his money. Every morning, the boy hugged his sister. He had three lovely horses. His wife went to the barn one day and killed the best horse. Her husband was working on the farm. She went to the door and cried for him and her father to come home. Her husband said, "What's the matter?"

His wife replied, "Your sister, that you are so fond of, that you hug every morning—go see what she did in the barn."

Her husband went to the barn only to find his horse with his head cut off. His wife thought he would punish his sister for killing his horse.

He said, "I have plenty of horses. If I need another one, I'll go get one."

This didn't suit his wife at all. One year after they were married, she had a baby—a little boy. When the baby was only three months old, the cutest little baby, she was still so jealous that her husband hugged his sister, that she used the same knife that she used to kill the horse, to cut off her son's head. She once again ran to the door screaming for her husband and her father to come home. She was tearing her hair out—completely beside herself. She had pushed her sister-in-law in a room, thrown the knife in with her and locked the door. When her husband and father arrived, they asked, "What's the matter, what happened?"

She replied, "Your sister that you are so fond of, who killed your horse about a year ago, go see in the cradle what she has done now. She has cut off your son's head. I pushed her into her room and locked the door so she can't get out."

Her husband went to the cradle. His son had bled to death. He opened the door to the room where his sister was. She got down on her knees and swore that she never touched the knife that killed his horse and his son.

He said to her, "Shut up! You did this!"

He stuffed her mouth with a handkerchief and ordered, "Get dressed so I can go kill you in the middle of the forest." She got dressed all in black and brought along her prayer book.

When they arrived in the middle of the forest, maybe two hundred feet into the forest, they noticed a river that flowed. He tied his sister to a tree and said, "Now, you have two choices: either I take my gun and kill you instantly or I cut off both your arms and throw them into the river."

"Well," she said, "if I have my choice, cut off both my arms and throw them into the river. Tie my prayer book on the small trees that are in front of me so that when it gets windy, the wind will turn the pages. That way I can read the prayers one more time before I die."

He did this. When he started to leave towards home, she said to her brother, "On your way home, you will get a splinter in your left foot that will not heal until I get my two arms back so that I can take the splinter out."

When she finally got untied from the tree, she remembered hearing that if you get lost in the woods, you should find a river and follow it downwards. She followed the river down, down, down, and suddenly she found herself in a village—but she had her two arms cut off. She went to a hotel and asked the hotel manager for a room. The hotel manager said, "Yes, you can stay here. I pity you, with both arms cut off."

She couldn't work, not even dress herself. The hotel manager said, "I have enough servants, they can help you dress."

One day an officer arrived, and the hotel manager said to him, "Now, I have the most beautiful girl here in the hotel. She's recovered, has gained weight, but has both her arms cut off." The officer said, "I'd be curious to see her."

As it turned out, the officer was the King's son. He went to see the girl, found her so beautiful that he asked her hand in marriage. She replied, "What's the use? I have both my arms cut off. I can't even make my bed or cook."

"That makes no difference. If you want to marry me, I have plenty of money and can hire servants to do your work."

"Well," she said, "if you want to marry me like this, I'll marry you."

She married him. But the boy's mother—the

43

wife of the King—did not want the marriage. "You're marrying a girl you don't even know. Maybe she's a tramp or something."

"It makes no difference. I am marrying her for myself, not for you."

Good enough. He married her. When they had been married about a year (with his mother living in her house and her son in the other), the King's son had to return to war. After his departure, his wife had two baby boys. Two beautiful boys. The mother wrote a letter to her son who was at war and announced that his wife had delivered two black babies. The ugliest babies she'd ever seen. It was all a lie. He wrote back to his mother, asking her to have his wife and two black babies exiled in the forest, as he didn't want a wife who had an affair with someone else.

So the mother called upon two soldiers and ordered them to kill her son's wife and her children in the forest. She forged a letter as if it had come from her son, with the order to kill his wife. The two soldiers went to get her son's wife and her two children. They said to her, "Your husband has ordered that you be killed."

They handed over the letter that was supposed to have been written by her husband, asking them to kill his wife and two children.

She asked, "How is it possible that he is not the father of the boys? No other man on this earth has had anything to do with me, only my husband."

The soldiers replied, "Well, we know that

they resemble their father, but he ordered us to do this, we have to."

She grabbed her babies and put one under each armpit. When they had gone quite a distance, one soldier said to the other, "It's awful to kill a disabled woman. If she promises to never tell on us, I'll put her in exile in the forest with her two babies."

She answered, "If you let me live, I promise to never leave the forest."

All right. They let her go.

In order to go into the forest, you had to cross a bridge. There was a guard on the bridge and you had to pay fifty cents to cross over. Although she was the wife of the King's son, she didn't have a penny. The guard wouldn't let her cross the bridge.

The river was low. She went to cross through the river in the water.... It was the same river where her brother had cut off her arms and thrown them in the water. She jumped on a rock in order to cross and she dropped the baby she held on her right into the water. She leaned over to pick up the baby—and grabbed her right arm. Her right arm was back in its place. She used it as if it had never been cut off. She made the same gesture with her left arm. She dropped the baby she held on her left side. She grabbed her left arm and put it back in its place. She found herself with both arms again. She then crossed over. She went back to the hotel and asked the hotel manager for a room. He said, "Yes, you can stay here."

She said, "I don't have a cent."

"It makes no difference. You can stay." The next morning, he said, "You can stay here with your two babies."

She stayed at the hotel for three years. After three years, her husband returned home from the war. He asked his mother what she'd done with his wife. She did not tell him that she'd ordered her killed. "You asked that she be exiled," she said, "and that's what I did."

"Well," he said, "if you ordered her to be exiled, it's possible that she is still living. Do you know which soldiers put her in exile?"

"Yes."

"Have them sent here."

The soldiers were brought to him. The King's son asked, "Did you kill my wife?"

"No, we were not able to kill her. We put her in exile. Your mother had ordered us to kill her, but we didn't. With both her babies, we put them in exile in the forest."

"Well then," the King's son said, "it's possible they're still living."

He started to search from place to place, country to country, to find his wife. It just happened that he went to the hotel where she was staying. He asked the manager if there was a woman staying there with both her arms cut off and two babies that would be about three years old. The manager replied, "Yes, there is a woman here with two babies about three years old, but she has both her arms."

The King's son answered, "Well then, it's not

her. But in any case, could I see her?"

He said, "Yes."

The manager went to show him the woman—but it was the portrait of his wife. She did not want to be recognized by him for fear he would have her killed. The King's son returned to spend the night at another hotel. He dreamed that he should return to the hotel the next morning as it was really his wife staying there. She saw him coming. She said to her two sons (who were talking now; they were three), "Quick, Papa is coming. If he comes into this room, you should both say together, 'Good day, Papa.'"

The father of the boys knocked on the door and entered. She said, "Good day," and he replied, "Good day to you."

"Good day, Papa," the boys cried.

The father asked, "Why are these children calling me Papa?"

She said, "You can't deny it. They're the picture of you."

He replied, "Yes, but you—you look so much like my wife when we were married. But you had your arms cut off. Today you have both your arms."

"Well, yes," she said. "By the grace of God, I got my arms back from the river where my brother had cut my arms off and thrown them into the river. I grabbed my arms and put them back into their place." She told him the whole story.

With that, the King's son was even happier that he had married her—she had her two arms. He brought her to his castle and had his mother come there. He said, "Mother, you ordered two soldiers to kill my wife and two children, that I wasn't their father. That wasn't the truth. They were not two black babies like you wrote in the letter." He took the letter out to show it to her. "Here's the letter you sent to me."

He had his mother punished. He had her put in prison for twelve years for having done all this.

His wife said, "Now, my brother is still in bed with a splinter in his left foot. I have to go there."

They hitched up the team of horses and went there. When they arrived, they asked her brother's wife, the farmer's daughter, if her husband was home. She answered, "Yes, he's at the house. He's laid up in bed with a splinter in his left foot. This happened one day while he was hunting in the forest." (She lied about this as he had really gone in the forest to kill his sister.)

"Can we see him?"

She replied, "Yes."

He had become very thin, nothing but skin and bones. She asked him, "What's the matter?"

He answered, "Well, when I returned home, you said that I would get a splinter in my foot and that it wouldn't heal until you took it out."

She replied, "Well, it's me, your sister!"

So sure enough, he stretched his foot out and she took out the splinter. After fifteen days, it was all healed.

Then, the King's son and his wife returned to the castle. I haven't received any other news since.

5. The Stingiest King in the World

Le Roi le plus avare du monde

The authoritative and humiliating pranks played by Ti-Jean are numerous and greatly appreciated by the storytellers, often involving humour which is a bit harsh. This tale,[1] which is similar to Type 1544, *The Man who Got a Night's Lodging*, is no exception, and the storyteller does not spare much at times. A King wants three rabbits for a feast he is putting on. He pays an exorbitant amount to a young man who has already conned the Queen and Princess.

This tale is found as much in the Scandinavian and Slavic countries as in Europe and Asia.[2] This one is the only version recorded in Acadia.[3] This story is a good introduction to the next one, "The Three Rabbits."

The Stingiest King in the World

ONCE THERE WAS A KING, the most miserly in the world. In his country, a law was passed that every year he had to give a supper that cost one thousand dollars. The parish gathered all the people so that it would cost one thousand dollars. This did not suit the King at all. It didn't please him to have to pay one thousand dollars for a supper. The others—the rich ones—told him, "If you can find three rabbits" (there were rabbits in that country) "to make a fricot, we will give you five hundred dollars."

Well, you can imagine how he worked towards saving five hundred dollars. On Monday morning, he left with his gun and said to his wife and daughter, "I will be back in three days. I'll return on Wednesday evening."

But Monday night, on the road in front of the King's castle, a young man was walking with three rabbits on his shoulder. The King's daughter said, "Mama, let's buy the rabbits. Chances are that Papa will not kill any as they're very rare. If you buy these three, it will save him five hundred dollars."

She hollered to him, "Come over here! You have to sell us your three rabbits. I will give you one hundred dollars for them."

This would have saved the King four hundred dollars.

"No, no, no. But you can have them for nothing if you want them."

"Ah well," she said, "what is this? You'll give them away? But we can't have them for one hundred dollars? How's that?"

"Well," he replied, "if you'll go to bed with me tonight, and if tomorrow night I can sleep with your daughter, I will give you the three rabbits. "

"Well," the daughter said, "Mama, if you're

50

game, I'm all for it, as this will save Papa five hundred dollars."

She thought only of the money, as miserly as her father. So the first night, Monday night, the wife slept with him. Tuesday night, the daughter. The next morning after breakfast, he put the three rabbits on his shoulder and went out the door. The King's wife said, "Hey, listen here. You promised to give us the three rabbits if I slept with you, and then my daughter—and now you're leaving with them?"

"Yes."

He then turned around asking the women, "What would you prefer? To leave you the three rabbits and go tell the King that the night before last I slept with you and that last night I slept with your daughter, or that I take my rabbits with me and nobody but us will know? "

They were caught. She said, "Well, if you're a guy like that, get the hell out of here with your three rabbits!"

So he took off. He was not ten feet from the castle when he met up with the King. The King said, "Can you sell me your three rabbits?"

"No, I cannot sell them."

The King said, "I will give you one hundred dollars."

"Well," he said, "give me one hundred dollars and pull your pants down so that I can beat your bottom until I draw blood." (He had a large needle to punch leather.) "I will scratch your bottom until you bleed. Then I will give you my three rabbits."

The King replied, "No, I won't be able to make it home."

He said to the King, "It won't kill you but it will hurt you."

"All right!"

Well, the King pulled his pants down, got his bottom all scratched up and bloodied and paid the one hundred dollars. When he got home, his daughter noticed that he was walking strangely, could hardly move. She said to her mother, "Mama, those are the three rabbits we earned."

The King heard this. He went to the house, walking all crooked, had his three rabbits. He got out his pistol and called out to his wife and daughter asking, "You have to tell me how you earned these three rabbits."

His wife replied, "But we didn't earn these three rabbits. I believe these are some that you bought or killed yourself."

He said to his wife, "No! When I approached the castle, I heard my daughter say, 'Mama, those are the three rabbits we earned.' Tell me how you earned these rabbits. Look at my bottom, look at the state I'm in—and I had to pay one hundred dollars for them."

They didn't want to talk, so he took his pistol out and said to his wife, "I'm going to shoot you, then my daughter." Well, they had no choice but to declare themselves.

The wife said, "Well, to get the three rabbits,

the night before last, I slept with him and last night our daughter. And then he took off with the three rabbits."

Well, the King was in a rage. He saddled up his best horse and left. He couldn't go very fast because he was so sore.

Meanwhile, this was the month of August and there was an old Negro woman working at making haystacks. She was approached by the young man who said to her, "Here comes the King after me. Just squat down. I will cover you with hay. Then I will put my hand in the haystack." Then he disguised himself.

The King arrived and asked, "Did you see a young man pass by on this road?"

The King didn't recognize the young man beside the haystack.

He said to the King, "I saw a young man but he was running with all his might."

"Ah!" the King said. "It's me that's chasing him. He played a trick on me."

He said to the King, "At the rate you're going and the rate he's going, you'll never lay a hand on him."

The King replied, "How much would it cost me to have you jump on my horse and go catch him for me?"

"Well, I can't. You see, I was on my way to the city to sell a barrel of oil when the sun started heating it up. I had to put my finger in the bung so that it doesn't boil over, so that I don't lose it."

The King said, "Well, how about if I put my finger in the bung and you...."

"Ah well, if you want to do that, all right."

The King came up to the haystack, put his finger in the old Negro woman's rear thinking it was in the oil barrel, while the young man jumped on the horse and left.

When the Negro woman felt the young man was far enough away to be safe, she started moving around under the hay. The King was scared and backed off. The hay covering her fell over—what did he see? An old Negro woman!

Well, the King was very angry. The young man had got one hundred dollars for the three rabbits. He had slept with his wife and daughter, and also had his best horse and saddle.

Anyway, the King returned to his castle. They made a fricot with his three rabbits. He still ended up with four hundred dollars anyway!

We were there, me and Nanette. It was the best fricot I ever tasted in my life!

6. The Three Rabbits

Les Trois Lapins

A King has promised his daughter's hand in marriage to the one who will bring her the finest fruit in the world. P'tit Jean succeeds at this feat. To try and lose him, the King submits P'tit Jean to a test. P'tit Jean ends up the winner and also humiliates a rival prince and the King himself.

This tale[1] of Type 570, *The Rabbit-herd* or *The Sack of Truth*, is completed with part of Tale-Type 850, *The Birthmarks of the Princess*. It depicts the intelligence and slyness of our hero P'tit Jean.

This tale is widespread around the world. We find about thirty versions collected in Canada,[2] of which three were in Acadia. This is the only one from Nova Scotia.[3]

The Three Rabbits

THE TALE OF THE THREE RABBITS is about a King who had a daughter and he wanted her to get married. She wasn't getting married.

There was also a widow who had three sons. The oldest was Henri, the second son was called Georges and the youngest was called P'tit Jean. They saw in the newspaper that the King wanted his daughter to get married. "Well, Mama," said Henri, the widow's oldest son, "I'm going to go see the King's daughter tomorrow morning."

Henri left. When he arrived to see the King's daughter, the King said, "My daughter is in her room. For you to have my daughter's hand in marriage, you have to bring her the most beautiful fruit on earth."

Henri came up with a potato. The King's daughter said, "Get out of here, you with your potato!"

She had him condemned and sent to prison. That night, the widow's other two sons said, "Mama, why isn't Henri coming home? He must have been sent to prison."

Georges said, "I'm going to go tomorrow morning." He brought an apple to the King's daughter.

She said to Georges, "Get out of here, you with your apple! I don't want to see your face. Off to prison."

But the third morning, P'tit Jean said, "Mama, now I'm going."

He left and when he got to a certain place, he had to go through a meadow. In that meadow there was an old Negro woman who had a sheep stuck in the mud. She asked P'tit Jean to save her sheep. P'tit Jean replied, "I can't. I'm on my way to go see the King's daughter and I'll get my shiny shoes all dirty. Well, guess I'll just have to take off my shoes and go barefoot."

He took his shoes off and went to get the woman's sheep. She then asked P'tit Jean, "What are you bringing to the King's daughter?"

P'tit Jean said, "I'm bringing her a plum, the most beautiful plum that I found in our garden."

The old woman said, "Well, give it to me."

He gave the plum to the old Negro woman. She passed the plum through her fingers, then gave it back to him. When P'tit Jean arrived to see the King's daughter, the King looked at the clock and said, "You only have five minutes left."

P'tit Jean entered the room. The King's daughter was on her way out. He showed her the plum. Oh, God! She found the plum so beautiful she said, "Papa! Mama! Come here. Look, the most beautiful plum that the widow's son brought for me."

The King and Queen went to see and sure enough the King said, "Yes, my daughter, it's a beautiful plum—but you're stuck marrying P'tit Jean. I have to do what I said I'd do."

The King's daughter said, "Papa, I will most certainly not marry P'tit Jean. I knew the widow's son and didn't want to see him."

The King replied, "I can't do that. I promised, and you have to marry P'tit Jean."

Well, the King thought he had found a way to get rid of P'tit Jean. He told him, "My daughter has three rabbits. I'm going to give them to you. I have a small cabin on the mountain with a nice yard. You're going to put the three rabbits in the yard and there's enough food in the cabin for a year. I'll give you one year. After a year and a day, you must return with the three rabbits in as good a shape as today. Otherwise, you will be hanged beside my castle."

"Well," P'tit Jean said, "you make the laws of this country. I'm obliged to do what you've just ordered."

The King gave him his daughter's three rabbits and brought him to the cabin on the mountain, where there was plenty of food. After six months had passed, the King said to the Prince (whom the King's daughter was seeing at the time), "You should go see P'tit Jean. It's possible that he'll still have the three rabbits, that he'll marry my daughter and you'll have nothing."

The Prince went to see P'tit Jean. He said, "Good day, P'tit Jean."

P'tit Jean said, "Good Day, Prince."

The Prince asked him, "Do you still have the three rabbits that belong to the King's daughter?"

"Yes."

"Could I see them?"

"Yes."

The Prince said, "You have to give me one."

"Ah, no. But," P'tit Jean said, "if you want, I'll let you earn one."

"Yes? How?"

"Well," P'tit Jean said, "there's an old horse that died next to the cabin, it's all decayed. If you want to haul the horse to the river with your teeth, piece by piece, I'll give you a rabbit."

"If the Queen and the King's daughter knew this, they'd never want to see my face again."

"Otherwise, you won't have a rabbit."

Ah! The prince thought to himself, "I'm going to do this." Sure enough. He had quite a hard time, but P'tit Jean ended up giving him a rabbit. Meanwhile, P'tit Jean had trained the rabbits to come to him when he'd whistle. When the Prince walked away with the rabbit underneath his arm, P'tit Jean let out a whistle and the rabbit escaped from the Prince, returning to P'tit Jean. He put the rabbit back in its cage. The Prince returned home and the King asked him, "What did you see?"

The Prince replied, "P'tit Jean is there, red and fat, with a beard down to here, but I didn't see any rabbits." (He was telling a lie. He had gotten a rabbit but the rabbit escaped.) "He told me that only you could get a rabbit."

The King said, "I'm going to go."

When the King arrived at P'tit Jean's, he asked him, "Do you still have my daughter's three rabbits?"

"Yes."

"Can I see them?"

"Yes."

"Ah!" the King said, "you have to give me one."

"Oh, no," P'tit Jean said. "But if you want, I can let you earn one. For six months I have been relieving myself in a barrel, and now it's full. If you want to haul this to the river, with your mouth, your teeth, I will give you a rabbit."

"Ah!" the King said, "if the Queen and my

daughter knew of this, I could never return to my castle."

P'tit Jean said, "Well, you won't get a rabbit."

Well, the King started his task. He hauled and hauled until he almost had a heart attack. P'tit Jean gave him a rabbit and when the King was gone a little way, P'tit Jean whistled, the rabbit escaped and returned to him. He put the rabbit in the yard.

When the King returned home, his daughter asked him, "What did you see?"

The King told her a lie: "P'tit Jean is red and fat, with a beard down to here, and he told me it would take you to obtain a rabbit."

When there was only one month left to make up the year, and the girl would have to marry P'tit Jean, she went to see him. The King's daughter said, "Can I have a rabbit?"

P'tit Jean answered, "Yes, you can have a rabbit. But only if you agree to lay down with me all day long in the shade of those big trees. Do this, and tonight I will give you a rabbit."

She replied, "No, no, no, no! I will not lay down with you under the big trees."

"You don't want to lay down with me today, but at the end of a year and a day, if I still have the three rabbits, you will have to sleep with me for the rest of your life. This, because your father promised me your hand in marriage."

Well, the King's daughter was stuck. She had no choice. She lay down with P'tit Jean. And when it came time for her to go, he gave her a rabbit. She went a little way and P'tit Jean whistled. The rabbit once again escaped and returned to him.

When the King's daughter got back to the castle, her father asked, "What did you see?"

"Well," she said, "P'tit Jean is there but I couldn't get a rabbit."

She had also told a lie. This made three lies told in the King's castle. Yes, but at the end of a year and a day, who arrives at the King's castle? P'tit Jean and his three rabbits.

P'tit Jean said to the King, "Here, Mr. King! Aren't these rabbits as nice as when you gave them to me?"

"Yes."

The King's daughter said, "Papa, I will not marry P'tit Jean."

The King said, "Well, you're stuck. I promised, and it will happen. But tonight, all three of you will sleep in the same bed. P'tit Jean in the back, you in the middle, and the Prince in the front. Tomorrow morning, at seven o'clock, I will come and unlock the door. If you're facing the Prince, you'll marry him. If you're facing P'tit Jean, you'll marry him."

All right! So all three of them went to bed. During the night, P'tit Jean needed to urinate. There was nowhere for him to go, no toilet, nothing. He returned to bed and held back. Around four o'clock, the Prince woke up with a bad case of cramps. He got up, looked around, the door was locked—no use. He asked P'tit Jean, "What am I going to do?"

P'tit Jean answered, "Well, I also needed to relieve myself, but I had to hold back and go to bed."

The Prince said, "Well, I can't hold back." The Prince laid down, he had diarrhea, out it came. He soiled the bed. He soiled the King's daughter. The King's daughter was asleep. All of a sudden, she woke up to a horrible stink. Meanwhile, P'tit Jean had a bottle of musk oil which he spread all over his body. The King's daughter turned towards P'tit Jean. Ah! he smelled so good that she grabbed him around the neck.

The King unlocked the door. The Prince got up and went into the corner of the room, his head down low. He was soiled from one end to the other. The stink hit the King's nose and he said, "What is that?"

The Prince answered, "Excuse me, Mr. King, I had an accident."

The King said, "You call this an accident. The state you're in, I call this being a bloody pig." He then said to P'tit Jean, "Get up. Let's deal with him."

They opened the window. They were on the third floor. They dropped the Prince from the window. P'tit Jean had the princess by the neck. She had to marry P'tit Jean. The Prince had to go home, and P'tit Jean married the King's daughter!

7. The Three Burned Children

Les Trois Enfants brûlés

This tale relates to the major theme of parents who want to get rid of their children. Type 327E, *Abandoned Children Escape from Burning Barn*, frames Type 326A*, *Soul Released from Torment*, closely related to Tale-Type 326, *The Youth Who Wanted to Learn What Fear Is (Jean sans peur)*, who was not scared when he spent the night in the castle, which allowed him to save a wandering soul. According to Aarne-Thompson, there are only seven versions of this tale: two from Ireland, five from French Canada.[1]

The only two versions recorded in Acadia came from Cheticamp in Nova Scotia, this one told by Marcellin Haché[2] and the other one, *L'Histoire de la grange*, told by Jean Z. Deveau.[3] The two differ only at the episode of the haunted house. In Mr. Deveau's version, the ghost is the soul of a man who has been murdered. For his bravery, the hero inherits his fortune. In Mr. Haché's version, the ghost is the soul of a man who has given himself to the devil. Having been able to spend the night in this house without being scared, our hero liberates the man from the devil and thus inherits his fortune.

The Three Burned Children

THIS IS A STORY ABOUT THREE BURNED CHILDREN. There was a man and his wife who had three sons, who were very bright, very intelligent. They had to support these children, pay their way through school and buy their clothing. This was very costly.

One day the man said to his wife, "If you want to go along with me, we're going to get rid of those three children. They cost us a lot of money."

The man had a large farm with two big barns. He had thought of burning one of the barns because it was old. During the summer, since it was so hot, they were in the habit of putting a bed in the old barn and the children would sleep there.

One night the farmer said to his wife, "We're going to get the children to sleep in the barn tomorrow night. It's hot and they'll go to sleep there. We'll start a fire in the barn. The people will think that the children set the fire and burned to death."

But the youngest of the three boys wasn't asleep. He overheard his father tell his mother about the fire. The next evening, when it came time to go sleep in the barn, the two older sons were excited about sleeping in the barn, but the youngest did not want to go. His father said to him, "Why don't you want to go? You've gone before."

He replied, "Last night I heard you tell Mama that tonight you were going to have us sleep in the barn so you could set it on fire and have us burned."

His father said, "You dreamed this. I had to wake you up because you were dreaming. Surely you see that it's not true."

Well, they cajoled him enough that he agreed to go to the barn. The two oldest boys fell asleep. But the youngest couldn't sleep. He kept thinking about this. Ah! Yes, soon the barn was on fire! He woke up his two brothers. They went to the doors. All the doors were locked. There was no way out. They were stuck there. They screamed for help but nothing. They went to a door that was used to throw out the animals' manure. All three of them pounded on the door until they busted it. They got out. The two oldest boys wanted to tell their father to come out, that the barn was on fire.

But the youngest son said, "No! It was Papa and Mama who wanted to have us burn in the barn. Look, we're intelligent and old enough to take care of ourselves. We're going to go on the road and try to make a life for ourselves."

So they left. Soon they found three roads, one that went to the left, one to the right and one that just kept on straight. The youngest asked his two brothers, "What are we going to do? Are we going to continue on the same road, all three of us, or are we going to separate?"

"Well," they answered, "you're the youngest, we'll take your advice."

"Well," he said, "my advice would be that one of you take the road going left, the other take the road going right, and I'll continue going straight."

The brothers replied, "All right!"

They promised to meet after a year and a day to see if they'd made any progress.

The youngest walked all day and found nothing. But when it was dark, he saw a light, and went over there. To the left of the road was a big three-story house, all lit up, and to the right, another house. He went to the house on the right. When he got there, he knocked on the door. A man told him to enter. He asked the man, "Can I sleep here and have some food? I'm starved. I haven't eaten since last night."

"Ah!" the man said, "you poor guy! I can't give you any food. You know, in this country there was a law passed that you cannot give any food to anyone. You'll have to go to the castle to the left of the road. There you will have all the food you want."

"Ah well," he said, "if I can't get any food here, I will go there."

The man then said, "Well, I'm going to tell you what's going to happen. If you go there, you'll be the tenth guy to sleep there and the next morning—they're dead."

He replied, "Well, I'd just as soon die in the castle as die out on the road. I cannot go any further."

So they went to the house. The man locked the door behind the boy, who went into the kitchen. There was a table in the middle of the floor, a big pot on the stove, two plates on the table—but nobody there. Nobody. The two plates filled themselves up. When this was all ready, two chairs rose and placed themselves at the table. He sat at the table, ate until he was full. The other plate was emptying itself the same as his, but nobody was there. He soon felt like going to bed. A door opened and there was a beautiful bed. The covers rose and he went and laid down.

He couldn't sleep. All of a sudden, he heard some noise coming from the third floor. He could hear the noise coming down the stairs. When the sound reached ground level, his door opened and he saw a man covered in flames coming towards him. He knelt in the bed. He had a bottle of holy water on him, took it out and made the sign of the cross with holy water on the bedroom floor and said, "Do not come any closer. The Good Lord is between you and me."

Sure enough, the sound started to go away until he couldn't hear it anymore, but soon the castle was filled with smoke. He got up, opened the door and windows in order to let the smoke out. He went to eat breakfast, only this time nothing was prepared for him. He had to make his own breakfast. There was plenty of food. The man who had brought him to this house came back to do what he'd always done before. He would come to the house and gather the dead bodies. Everyone who had slept there before would die. Instead, he found the boy sitting beside the stove, smoking a cigarette.

"Good day! Why are you still alive this morning?"

He answered, "I didn't believe what you told me last night. I ate, went to bed and slept all night."

The man said, "I know more about this than you do. You pulled through but not without being scared."

"Well," he said, "yes."

The man said, "It's my brother who gave himself to the devil for money. To be set free, someone had to sleep here and still be alive in the morning. You have liberated him from the devil. You have inherited his fortune. You inherit his money and gold. He was a millionaire!"

A year and a day from when the three brothers had separated, he said to the man, "I have to go find my brothers."

He hitched up a team of horses and off he went. When he arrived, his two brothers were waiting for him. He asked them, "Did you make any progress?"

"No, nothing."

"Well," he said, "come with me. I have enough money and gold for the three of us!"

He brought them to his castle where there was lots of money and gold.

He then said to his brothers, "How would you like to go see our mother and father, to see how much better off they are after the fire?"

They all agreed.

He hitched up a double team of horses and took his brothers to visit his mother and father. They could hardly recognize the place. The big house gone; the huge barn gone; the farm—there was very little left. There was a small shed with a pipe sticking out of the roof, a bit of smoke rising from it. They went into the shed and saw their mother and father and said, "You're here?"

They didn't recognize their sons. The mother and father replied, "Yes, the Good Lord is fair, we've been punished."

"Well," the youngest son said, "we're very rich and we'd love to have some elderly people with us, that we can take care of."

"Well, if you want to take us with you, we'll go."

So sure enough, they all went back to the castle. They sat down at the table, the whole bunch, for supper. When they had had their supper, the youngest of the three said, "I'd like to hear stories from the old days."

"Ah!" the father said, "I have a story to tell you but it's almost too terrible."

"Well," he said, "it's those type of stories we would like to hear."

The father said, "Well, we had three sons who went to school. They were very smart but they cost us so much. One night, we put them in our barn and set it on fire. The Good Lord punished us. Everything I attempted to do, failed. I lost my house, barn and farm because I couldn't pay my debts. All that they left me was my old shed."

"Ah!" the youngest son said, "that's terrible, burning your own children, eh?"

The father replied, "Yes. It certainly was terrible."

"Your three sons, if you saw them now, would you know them?"

"Oh," he said, "yes."

The old woman spoke: "Yes, especially the youngest one, I loved him so much!"

"Well," the son replied, "I am the youngest of your three boys and these are my two brothers. We didn't burn in the fire, we got away."

Well, they found that so tough, they were so old, that they both took sick, the old man and old woman. Within fifteen days, they were both dead. I believe it was Méderic[4] that dug up their graves.

8. A Thousand Dollars for a Dozen Eggs

Mille piastres pour une douzaine d'œufs

This Tale-Type[1] 821B, *Chickens from Boiled Eggs*, is widely known from the Caucasus region to Italy, in Europe and in the Scandinavian and Slavic countries.[2]

A woman provides lodging for a priest and his mother. Twenty years later, she sends him a bill in the amount of one thousand dollars for the eggs she'd served them during their stay. At the trial, a young man manages to free the priest through his sharp reasoning.

One Thousand Dollars for a Dozen Eggs

THERE WAS A PRIEST who was in a parish that was poor. Poor. The bishop transferred him to another parish that was even poorer than the one he'd left behind, and he couldn't get there in one day.

He left with his horse and wagon, bringing his mother with him. When evening came, they arrived at a house where the priest asked the woman there to lodge them for the night. The woman said, "Yes."

When they entered the house, the woman polished her stove and then fried up half a dozen

71

eggs, three for the priest and three for his mother. They had supper and stayed overnight. The next morning, the woman boiled a half dozen eggs, three for the priest and three for his mother. The priest was able to have breakfast because he was too far away from his new parish to say the morning mass. He would have to get there by evening.

That night, when they arrived at the church that he was to take under his wing, he saw a small glebe house, a small and poor church, but it was all very clean, very tidy.

The priest was there for twenty years, and one day received a letter from a lawyer. It was the lawyer of the woman who had provided lodging for him and his mother twenty years earlier. She was asking him to pay one thousand dollars for the dozen eggs she'd served them during their stay at her house.

She had calculated the eggs according to how many chickens she would have had if she had put the eggs under a hen to hatch. Twelve eggs, that would have made twelve chickens, twelve chickens.... She charged the amount it cost in those days for eggs, taking into consideration the number of roosters she would have had out of the bunch— these would add to the cost. So he had to get a lawyer.

The priest went to see a lawyer, one of the smartest around. He showed him the bill from the woman. The lawyer calculated everything— everything—and said, "I can't help you. She's nuts!

But she's made her calculations well, and you're stuck paying the one thousand dollars."

The priest asked, "How do you want me to pay one thousand dollars? I don't have a penny."

The lawyer said, "Well, I can't help you. It's no use for me to go to trial."

Well anyway, the day of the trial, the priest went. He was passing by a college. There were some students outside. One of them said, "The priest is going to trial but he's going to lose. I'd like to be his lawyer. I'd be able to save him."

The priest overheard this and asked, "What? You'd save me?"

"Yes."

"How?"

The student asked him, "What time does court open?"

"Well, it opens at ten o'clock."

"Just tell the judge I'll be there at ten minutes past ten o'clock."

All right.

The priest showed up and the woman was there with her lawyer. The judge asked the priest, "Don't you have a lawyer?"

The priest answered, "Yes, and he's not here yet. He told me he'd be here at ten minutes past ten o'clock."

"Ah!" the other lawyer said. "He certainly knew that we open at ten o'clock."

"Yes," the priest said, "but I didn't ask him why."

At ten minutes past ten, he arrived. The judge asked the priest, "Is this your lawyer?"

He said, "Yes."

"Why weren't you here at ten o'clock?"

The student answered, "Well, this morning my father wanted to sow his peas. But before sowing the peas, I had to boil them, and that held me up for ten minutes."

"Well," the judge said, "how come? Boiling peas before sowing them! The peas will not rise if they're dead."

"Well," the student said, "if the boiled peas are dead, the boiled and fried eggs will not hatch."

The judge turned towards the priest and said, "All you have to pay is twenty-five cents for the dozen eggs. That's all."

The woman lost the trial and had to pay the court's cost, and the priest was saved!

9. The Shrewd Thief

Le Fin Voleur

This tale[1] about Ti-Jean is of Type 1525A: *Theft of Dog, Horse, Sheet or Ring*; this is probably the best known and the most typical of French Canada. Ti-Jean, who had become a very subtle thief, has to undergo certain tests or ordeals submitted by the King, or otherwise he will be hanged. Ti-Jean, using tricks, confounds the King's plans and outsmarts the King by getting rich at his expense, and ends up marrying his daughter.

This tale is widespread in the Scandinavian and Eastern countries as well as in Europe, Oceania (the South Sea Islands), in America, in Japan,[2] and in French Canada and Acadia.[3]

A pattern of this tale is found in the next story, "The Most Beautiful Girl in the World." In the two tales, the hero asks, "Are you not the country's three thieves?"

The Shrewd Thief

THE STORY OF THE SHREWD THIEF. There was a widow who had three sons. The oldest son's name was Henri, the second son was Georges and the third son Jean—they would call him P'tit Jean.

They were very poor, a real charity case. Every day they had to go to the King for food.

One day the King said to the widow, "It seems to me that if your sons wanted to, they could find work and you wouldn't need charity every day."

Well, one morning the three sons told their mother, "We're going to leave, all three of us."

The three brothers left. They followed a wide road. All of a sudden they found themselves with three roads: their own, one to the right and one to the left. P'tit Jean, the youngest, asked, "What are we going to do? Are we going to continue the three of us on the same road, or are we going to separate?"

"Well," they answered, "you're the youngest and you appear to be the smartest, we'll take your advice."

P'tit Jean said, "My advice is that one of you take the road to my left, the other to my right, and that in a year and a day we return here to see who's made the most progress."

They said their good-byes and left. Henri didn't go very far before he stumbled upon a small village where he worked in carpentry. Well, it wasn't too bad. Georges found a small village where an old man worked in a forge. He asked the man if he'd hire him so he could learn the trade of a blacksmith. The man said, "Yes."

Good! It still wasn't too bad.

P'tit Jean walked all day. That night he came to a cabin at the edge of the woods, a large cabin about forty foot square with a small window. He looked in the window and saw three men. He knocked on the door and they said, "Come in." He entered and they asked, "What are you doing here?

We've been here for forty years and you're the first person who's come here."

It occurred to him that these were three thieves.

P'tit Jean asked, "Are you the three thieves of this country?"

They replied, "Yes."

"Good," he said. "I'm right where I want to be." (It was fear making him say this.) "I went to school for three years to learn my trade as a thief. I'm one of the wisest thieves of all."

One of the thieves said, "Well, you're just the man we need. It's been a few days since we stole anything."

Well, the next morning all four of them had to separate and return to the cabin by three o'clock. The three thieves returned with nothing at all. They hadn't found anything and they had very little to eat. P'tit Jean came back with a quarter of beef.

The thieves asked P'tit Jean, "Where did you get that?"

"Ah, never mind," he said. "Just eat!"

They roasted the quarter of beef. It was so good. P'tit Jean said, "This is nothing; wait until tomorrow."

The next day, they all left again. P'tit Jean found a man who was slaughtering a pig. They chatted for quite a while, then the man hung the pig in his store and went into his house. P'tit Jean grabbed a chunk of pork and took it to the thieves.

"Well, look!" they said. "Aren't you smart!"

"Oh well," he said, "I told you, I learned my trade as a thief."

Well, this went on for a year. After a year and a day, he was a shrewd thief and stole most anything. He said to the other thieves, "When I left, I promised my two brothers I'd meet up with them again."

"Ah well," they said, "then go."

When he got to the meeting place, his brothers were waiting for him. "Well, Henri," he said, "did you learn anything?"

"I learned the carpentry trade. Our mother has been living in an old house for a long time; we need to repair it." He said, "I'm going to build a beautiful house."

"And you, Georges?"

"Well," he said, "I learned the trade of blacksmith."

Henri and Georges then asked their brother, "And you, P'tit Jean?"

P'tit Jean answered, "Ah, me! I won't tell you."

"You don't want to tell us, but we told you."

"Well," P'tit Jean said, "I'm going to tell you, but you can't tell anyone. I learned the trade of a shrewd thief."

"Oh well," they replied, "it's quite simple—you'll be hanged."

"Well," he said, "don't say anything, and nobody will know."

They went to their mother's house. There was

nothing to eat for dinner. She had to go see the King for food. The King said to the widow, "Ah! Your sons have returned."

"Yes."

"Did they learn anything?

She said, "Henri learned the carpentry trade."

"Well," the King said, "he's going to make a living here in this country. There'll be work for him." The King then asked, "What about Georges?"

She answered, "Georges, he learned the blacksmith trade."

"Ah, well," the King said, "that's even better. If he doesn't have enough money to build a forge, I will build one for him. I have enough work for him, he can make a living."

"Well, that's great!"

"But," the King then said, "I heard that P'tit Jean learned the trade of a shrewd thief. That's quite a situation, to have a thief in our country. It's a very frightening thing! Well," he said, "I'm going to test him. I have six soldiers who bake bread for my pigs. I'm going to have them cook some nice white bread for the pigs. The soldiers will stand guard. If P'tit Jean cannot steal the bread, he will be hanged beside my castle."

The widow went home and explained this to P'tit Jean. "Good!" He said, "Mama, for the longest time we've been eating the King's black bread. Tomorrow we will eat the white bread that the King throws to the pigs."

She said, "It's quite simple—you're going to be killed. You're not going to be able to steal from them, six soldiers with guns on their shoulders standing guard."

The King told his soldiers that there were three pigs in the forest, two white and a black—a big black sow. Then he said, "When the pigs come here for bread, let them take it away. It was baked for them."

P'tit Jean went into the forest, found the black sow and killed it. He skinned it, keeping the ears, the nose, the mouth, the hoofs and the hide of the sow to make a disguise for himself. Then he went on all fours, with the big ears. The soldiers thought it was the King's black sow and said, "Here, take the bread. The King said, 'We must let her take the bread to the rest of the pigs in the forest.'"

But P'tit Jean brought the bread home. The next morning when his mother got up, he said to her, "Here, Mama, eat the King's white bread today and put the black bread aside."

Meanwhile, the King was out checking on his pigs. He found his big black sow killed on the side of the trail. All the meat was there but the hide was gone. He asked his soldiers, "What did you do with my black sow?"

"Well, she came here, we let her take the bread."

The King said, "You are a bunch of imbeciles. It was P'tit Jean who killed my sow, skinned it and came here in disguise—and you didn't notice."

"Ah well," they said, "it's not our fault."

P'tit Jean said to his mother, "Go see what the King will have to say."

She went there, and the King said, "Ah! P'tit Jean stole my twelve loaves of bread. Can you tell him that at exactly midnight tonight, he is to go in my stable and steal my best horse and carriage. There will be six soldiers at the door of the stable, and six at the door of the carriage house. If he cannot steal this, he will be hanged at my castle's door."

P'tit Jean's mother told him all this. She also said, "You're going to be hanged at the King's castle tomorrow."

"Oh no, Mother!" he replied. "For how long now have you been going to see the King on an old horse? Tomorrow, you will visit the King with his horse and carriage."

He then went to see a seamstress and had her make him a missionary outfit: the whole ensemble with a huge rosary and a book. That night, it was raining. He paced back and forth in front of the stable. One of the soldiers said to another, "It's kind of strange, a missionary priest out in the rain on a night like this." Another soldier said, "Go ask him to come in for shelter."

The soldier went to him and said, "Good day, my dear Father."

He said, "Good day, my child."

"Why are you outside this evening?"

"Well," he said, "you know that I'm on a mission, and when I'm out on a mission I cannot stay at the glebe house."

"Well," the soldier said, "couldn't you come in the barn for shelter?"

"Yes. I can go in, but only if I'm asked. I cannot go in without being invited."

"Well, come in."

They went into the barn. They all sat in a corner and chatted away until ten o'clock. "Well," the missionary priest said, "I have to go to bed, I have to sleep."

"Go to bed in the corner."

"But," the priest replied, "I'm in the habit of taking a shot of rum before I go to bed."

"Ah! Go ahead."

The soldiers really wanted to have a drink but the priest drank everything that was in his flask. There wasn't much in it, only a shot.

The priest then asked them, "Would you like to drink some rum?"

"Yes."

He had slipped something in the rum to put them all to sleep. He gave each of the six soldiers a drink. They all fell asleep. Then he went into the barn and took the horse and carriage and went home.

When P'tit Jean's mother got up the next morning, he said to her, "Here, Mama, go visit the King with his horse and carriage." A beautiful horse, full of life.

When the soldiers woke up, the missionary

priest gone, the horse and carriage gone.... They said, "The missionary priest—it was really P'tit Jean, the widow's son, and we didn't realize."

The widow went to see the King once again to see what he had to say about all this. The King said, "He's going to ruin me. He stole my twelve loaves of bread, stole my horse and carriage. Just tell him that tonight at midnight, to go to the church to see the parish priest. There is five thousand dollars in a safe in his bedroom. He has to steal the money, and if he doesn't he will be hanged outside my castle."

When the widow told her son, P'tit Jean said, "Good, Mama. For a very long time you've been living in an old house that's not even finished on the inside. Henri, who's now a carpenter, is going to order some wood and build you a new house with the five thousand dollars from the parish. You're going to enjoy yourself, just wait and see."

P'tit Jean went over to get the King's ox that worked on the farm. He hitched up the ox and wagon, built a box and put it in the wagon. He went to the church, tied the ox to the fence next to the church and went inside. He started ringing the church bell, lit up all the lamps in the church. He continued to ring the bell and it woke up the priest. The priest asked his servant, "What's happening in the church? The bell is ringing and all the lamps are lit."

The priest's servant said, "I'm not going to go see what it is."

"Well," the priest said, "I have to go see. I have to see what's happened."

He went over to the church and found another priest singing the mass. He was dressed in his missionary outfit. He was wearing a huge white sheet over his back, and in big black letters it read, "Angel Gabriel, down from heaven, sent here by God." He turned toward the parish priest: "Are you the parish priest?"

He replied, "Yes."

"Well," he said to the priest, "I'm going to turn around and you're going to read what's written on my back."

He turned around and the priest read what was on his back. He turned back towards the priest and asked, "Did you read what was there?"

"Yes."

"What is it?"

"Well," the priest replied, "it says: 'Angel Gabriel, down from heaven, sent here by God!'"

"Yes, that's it." He said, "I've been sent here by God to bring you to heaven in body and soul just like the Virgin Mary, but with the parish's five thousand dollars that you have on hand."

"For that," the priest said, "I have to go to the glebe house."

"Well," he said, "hurry up. You only have a quarter of an hour left."

The parish priest went to the glebe house, took the five thousand dollars and said to his servant, "I'm bidding you good-bye. I'm on my way to

84

heaven in body and soul, like the Virgin Mary."

When he returned to the church, he gave the five thousand dollars to Angel Gabriel, who then said, "Now, come with me."

They went outside and he put the priest in the box in the back of the wagon. He had made holes in the cover of the box to give him some air. They left, galloping away. From time to time the priest would say, "It's hard going to paradise, body and soul, by wagon."

P'tit Jean said, "Ah yes, but as you know, the road to paradise is very rough."

"Ah well," he said, "yes."

P'tit Jean said, "Just endure it."

When they arrived at the King's castle, he tied the ox to the fence and left. He went home with the five thousand dollars.

The next morning when the King got up, he looked out his window and saw the ox hitched to a wagon containing a new box. He went to the box, and all a sudden it spoke, "It's hard to go to paradise, in body and soul, in a little wagon."

The King said to his soldiers, "Bring me my axe."

One of the soldiers took the axe and lifted the cover of the box. Who came out of the box? The parish priest. The king recognized him, but he said, "How is it that you are here?"

The parish priest answered, "How is it that I am here? Well, at midnight Angel Gabriel came into my church and he told me I had to get the five thousand dollars of the parish that I had on hand. He told me that he was going to bring me to heaven in body and soul by wagon, and he brought me here."

The King replied, "Angel Gabriel? That was P'tit Jean, the widow's son, that I had sent."

The priest said, "What? It was you that sent him?"

"Yes."

"Well," the priest then said, "if you sent him, you're going to have to pay me back the five thousand dollars." Then the priest went home.

P'tit Jean arrived home and said, "Here, Mother, five thousand dollars. Have a beautiful house built for yourself. You're really going to enjoy this. But you need to go see the King to find out what he says now."

The widow went to see the King. "Ah!" the King said to her, "P'tit Jean has ruined me. He stole my twelve loaves of bread, stole my horse and carriage, stole five thousand dollars from the priest that I had to repay. He has to come here right away!"

The King had a daughter. P'tit Jean went to see the King. The King said, "How much money will it take, so that I never have to see your face again or be bothered by you?"

"Well," P'tit Jean replied, "give me your daughter's hand in marriage and five thousand dollars, and I will never bother you again."

The King said, "I don't regret giving you five

thousand dollars, but for my daughter to marry you—that's up to her."

"Well, Papa," the King's daughter said, "I think P'tit Jean is pretty smart, and with his five thousand dollars from the parish and the other five thousand dollars from you, it makes ten thousand dollars. I believe that he's rich enough to support me."

Sure enough, she married P'tit Jean. He married the King's daughter, built a beautiful house, brought his mother and two brothers to live with them and they were very happy! I have not heard any other news of them.

10. The Most Beautiful Girl in the World

La Plus Belle Fille du monde

This tale,[1] Type 506B, *The Princess Rescued from Robbers*, is well known in Acadia where we have recorded more than ten versions.[2] It seems that certain tales teach us something about sharing, and in this one the hero proves that happiness can be found through generosity and giving.

The world's most beautiful girl, the King's daughter, is taken prisoner by three thieves and is freed by a widow's son. The thieves are looking for them and a woman hides them. In his hiding place, the boy discovers the corpses of their hostess's husband and son; she couldn't afford to bury them. The boy gives her the funds for a proper tomb. He is thrown into the sea by a captain who pretends to be the princess's saviour. The boy will be helped by the late husband and son whom he had paid to have buried. He will marry the princess, and the captain will be punished for his crime.

Even though they both have the same frame, this version from Marcellin Haché is totally different from the one collected by Gérald E. Aucoin from Jean Z. Deveau,[3] who was also originally from Cheticamp.

The Most Beautiful Girl in the World

THE MOST BEAUTIFUL GIRL IN THE WORLD was the daughter of the King of Paris. The King bragged about her to everyone. He announced that he had the most beautiful girl in the world in all newspapers printed throughout the universe. It wasn't long before governments from other countries responded to this and told the King that if he claimed to have the most beautiful girl in the world, he should send her from country to country so they could see if this was actually true. They would pay all her expenses and they'd give her fifty thousand dollars upon her return.

The King sure regretted having done this, now that his daughter had to leave home. They had set a date for her departure. She had no choice. She left promising her mother and father that she would send them a letter every month. This went fine for a year, but after the year was up there were no more letters!

She went from country to country, and everywhere she went she was the most beautiful girl. Finally they said to her, "There's an island with about forty families on it. If you go there and they find you to be the most beautiful girl in the world, you can then return to your home."

She made it to the island. She put up posters everywhere inviting all the beautiful girls to gather at a hall. She was again found to be the most beautiful girl. They told her, "Now you can go home. You are the most beautiful girl in the world!"

She then had to hire a steamboat to get off the island and cross over. Soon they encountered a storm, losing the entire crew. She managed to save herself. She climbed up a cliff. She saw that there were no houses, nothing but woods. She followed the side of the cliff until she suddenly came upon a trail in the woods, about four feet wide. She said to herself, "There must be people here." She started walking along the trail and went about two hundred feet, where she met up with three thieves. Apparently these thieves knew everything. They said to her, "You are the most beautiful girl in the world, who went from country to country to show that you are the most beautiful of all, but you will not go any further."

They captured her; she couldn't move. They brought her to their cabin and locked her up in a room. She had no means of unlocking the door. She was stuck there.

After two years without any news from her, her family said, "She must have been killed."

The King said that for anyone that wanted to search for his daughter, he would pay him all the money he wanted for the return of his daughter. He would also give him his daughter's hand in marriage and half of his fortune.

THERE WAS A WIDOW who had a son. He said to her, "Mama, I must go."

"Well," she asked, "why? The two of us have enough money."

"But it isn't the money that I want. It's the girl, the King's daughter."

Off he went, to all the countries the King's daughter had been to. When he arrived on the island where she'd been, they told him, "She was found to be the most beautiful girl on this island and then she left. She hired a steamboat and crossed over. They were lost."

The widow's son was aboard a steamboat that also lost its crew. But he saved himself on a piece of the boat's debris, and ended up on the same island on which the King's daughter was stranded. He took the same trail she did, and soon met up with the three thieves.

They said, "You're looking for the most beautiful girl in the world."

The widow's son acted surprised. He said, "I don't know what you mean. I've never heard of a girl that's called 'the most beautiful girl in the world.' Are you the three thieves of this country?"

"Yes."

"Well," he said, "I've studied my trade as a thief and I'm one of the best thieves there is."

"Well," they said, "come with us."

They took him to their castle but did not show him the girl. She was locked up in a room. It had an iron door so even if you would have had an axe, you couldn't break it down. The next morning, the four thieves had to go out and try to earn a living. They were to return to the castle by three o'clock. One of the thieves couldn't find anything to do, so he went to sleep. The widow's son wasn't a thief at all. He returned to the castle, made a mould of the key to the girl's room, went into the woods with a file and made a key for the room. The other thieves came upon the thief that was sleeping and woke him up. He said to them, "You shouldn't have woken me up. I was dreaming that the guy that's with us has made himself a key to the room, unlocked the door and taken off with the girl."

"Ah!" they replied, "believing in a dream!"

"Well," he said, "I'm sure it's true."

Sure enough. They returned to the castle and found the door open and the girl was gone.

"Ah! my dream—you thought it wasn't true."

The widow's son and the girl had walked all night. The next morning they came to a small house where a woman was on the veranda washing clothes in a tub. He said to the woman, "Could you hide us? We're being chased by three thieves."

She looked at her clock and answered, "Ah! There's only five more minutes until they pass this way." She then said to the widow's son, "You go hide in the basement. They won't go there." She said to the girl, "You go hide in the attic. They won't go there."

Yes, but when he went into the basement, he fell between two dead men. He thought to himself, "She gets them to hide here, the thieves come and kill them, then throw them in the basement."

92

Shortly after he hid himself, the thieves arrived and asked the woman, "Did you see a young man and a girl around here?"

She replied, "No. I've been out here washing clothes since daybreak, and you're the first people to pass by."

The thief that had the dream the night before said, "I told you they took the other road. You wouldn't believe me."

"Well," they said, "we're going to believe you."

They turned around and took the other road. When the woman thought that they were far enough, she said to the widow's son that was in the basement, "Come upstairs." She said to the girl, "Come down."

She prepared them a lunch. The widow's son, who believed that they were going to be killed any minute, said to the woman, "How come you have two dead men in the basement?"

"I'm going to tell you. It's my husband and my son that died from the fevers. In this country, people who have debts cannot be buried. My husband owes two hundred dollars in debts, and he will not be buried until the debts are paid. That is why you saw me this morning washing clothes in a tub. I take all the clothes I can find in the city to wash, to earn some money to pay the debt."

He asked the woman, "How much is the debt?"

"Two hundred dollars."

He reached into his pocket and handed the

woman two hundred dollars to pay off her husband's debt and two hundred dollars to bury her husband and her son.

The woman said, "I will not repay you. I won't be able to. But the good Lord will see that you are compensated later on."

The widow's son and the girl left and soon arrived in a city where the King of France's ship was docked. He went aboard and said to the captain, "What are you looking for with the King's ship?"

The captain replied, "I'm looking for the King's daughter."

He said, "I have her at the hotel."

"Well," the captain said, "go get her."

The widow's son left to get the girl. This situation didn't suit the captain at all. The King had told him that if he found his daughter, he'd be able to marry her. He told his crew, "This will not do. The widow's son is going to end up with the girl, and I'll end up with nothing." They all left to return home.

Around midnight, the captain said to the widow's son, "Come see the beautiful blue fish that are swimming by the ship."

The widow's son leaned over to see the blue fish, and the captain pushed him into the sea. It was dark, and they lost sight of him. The captain hollered to the girl that the widow's son, the one who had saved her life, was drowned. She came upstairs and wanted to throw herself into the sea with him. They stopped her and the captain said to the girl, "Now, he's drowned and that's that. You're going to tell your father that I'm the one who saved your life. Then I will be able to marry you and get half your father's fortune."

She didn't want this at all. The captain then said, "If you don't agree, your grave will be there. You'll be drowned too."

She was forced to promise that she'd go along with this. Meanwhile the widow's son, who was a very good swimmer, was still at sea. All of a sudden, he came upon a canoe. He got into the canoe. Shortly after, someone appeared from the sea. He asked to get in.

The widow's son replied, "Yes. Get in." Not long after, another. He said, "Get in."

The man said to the widow's son, "Do you know who we are?"

"No."

He then explained, "Do you remember the woman who helped you hide in the basement and the girl in the attic?"

"Yes."

"Well, I'm her husband and this is my son. You made such a generous gesture by paying my debt of two hundred dollars and paying two hundred dollars to have us buried that the Good Lord wouldn't permit you to perish here. All that you wish for in our name will be granted!"

"Well," the widow's son said, "I would like to be transported back to my country, Paris."

"Well," he said, "you will."

The widow's son fell asleep in the canoe. When he woke up, he was about ten feet from the King's wharf and the two men that were with him were gone. He tied his canoe to the wharf. It took eleven days for the ship with the girl aboard to return. On the eleventh day, they arrived. The captain asked the King, "Are you going to do what you promised? You said if I brought back your daughter I could have your daughter's hand in marriage and half your fortune."

"Yes," the King replied, "you will be married tomorrow."

There was a boy who heard the news and went over to tell the widow's son, "The King's daughter is getting married tomorrow. You're going to lose her. You're the one who saved her and you're going to lose her."

The widow's son put on his best clothes. He went and sat in the first row at the church. The King made a ring for his daughter and said, "This will be your wedding ring. Just place it upon the finger of the man who saved you—that's to say, the captain."

"Ah well," she said, "yes."

When the girl entered the church, she looked around. She saw the widow's son, the one who had saved her life! She didn't know how he had saved his own life. When the priest called out for the couple to come up to the altar, she grabbed the widow's son by his jacket and brought him to the altar. She placed the ring on his finger. The captain was left behind. When they got outside, the King said to his daughter, "What did you do? You went and married the widow's son?"

"But," she said, "Papa, you told me to place the ring upon the finger of the man who saved me. That wasn't the captain. It was the widow's son!"

"Well, why did you tell me last night that it was him?"

She answered, "To save my life, I had to say it. The captain told me my grave would be in the same place as the widow's son if I didn't agree."

"Ah well," he said, "name a punishment—and I will punish him."

"Put him in the same canoe that saved my life, two hundred miles out at sea with no oars. If he's as smart as I was, let him save himself."

So sure enough, they went and put him two hundred miles at sea.

11. The Fourteen Thieves

Les Quatorze Voleurs

This tale[1] of "The Fourteen Thieves" originates from Type 956B: *The Clever Maiden Alone at Home Kills the Robbers.* A young girl kills thirteen thieves by cutting off their heads one after the other. She fails to get the fourteenth one, who in spite of all his efforts, cannot exercise vengeance on her.

If sometimes in the tales, as in our traditional society, the woman has exercised a more or less very passive role confined to the household, she is often found in a dynamic role that is quite comparable to that of Ti-Jean's skills and exploits. This is the case in several tales in this collection.

The Fourteen Thieves

THE STORY OF THE FOURTEEN THIEVES is about a man who had a tannery. He had his family downstairs and his shop upstairs. One night when they all arrived at home, he had forgotten to lock the shop. He had three daughters and he said to the oldest, "You must go into the shop to lock up. The keys are under the counter, just lock the door."

The oldest daughter replied, "I'm not going. I'm too scared of thieves."

He asked the second daughter. She didn't want to go either. But the third daughter, the youngest daughter, had made a promise never to say no to her father, so when he asked her she replied, "I'll go. I'm scared but I will go just the same because I made a promise never to say no to you."

She left, going up the stairs to the shop. The keys were under the counter so she took the keys. When she got to the door to lock up, she saw fourteen thieves not far away. It was night time. She got very scared, staying by the door, not moving. They had made themselves a little campfire to make tea, not too far from the shop. While they were having their tea, the boss of the thieves said to one of the gang, "You should go see upstairs: it's possible that the owner might not have locked the shop."

The thief went up the stairs. The girl was still waiting, with a sword her father had given to her in case of emergency. When he got upstairs, he opened the door and she cut off his head with the sword. He fell down the stairs. After a while, the boss of the thieves said, "Go take a look. He must have gone in and isn't coming down."

The thief went to see and the same thing happened to him. She killed all thirteen. She'd cut their heads off and they'd fall downstairs. There was only the boss left. He went upstairs and the girl, who was so excited after killing thirteen thieves, only managed to cut off the flesh on top of his head. He looked down—his thirteen brothers dead, their heads cut off. Well, he had to get out of there.

The girl was so nervous, so scared, that when she went downstairs she went the wrong direction and got lost. Early the next morning, she came upon a nice little house in a small village. There was a woman on the veranda doing the wash. The girl asked the woman if she could keep her, and the woman agreed.

The girl said, "I'm dying of hunger."

The woman gave her some food. The girl then said, "I'd like to go to bed." She went to bed and fell asleep. While she was sleeping, the man of the house arrived. He was a boss in a factory. His daughter told him, "I have a girl here that arrived starved and wanting to go to bed."

When the girl got up, the man of the house asked the girl to tell her story and where she was from. She told him where she came from and that her father owned a tannery, that he had forgotten his keys, that she had to go lock up, that there were fourteen thieves in the area, that she had killed thirteen, and that the fourteenth—she had cut off the top of his head. "Well," the man said to the girl, "you did well. Fourteen thieves, bandits."

Anyway, the man put in the newspaper that the girl had killed thirteen thieves and that she had cut off the top of the head of the fourteenth thief. He also put the name of the house where the girl was staying.

The thief happened to buy the paper and saw this story. It told where the girl was. One day, he disguised himself and found an artist who made statues and said to him, "You must make a man-sized statue of the Virgin Mary." (The thief, he was a little man.) "I want you to make it deep enough that I can get into it. Make some holes, two for the eyes, the mouth, the nose to breathe, everything. I want you to paint the statue as a portrait of the Virgin Mary and then try to sell it for seventy-five dollars. But when you get to this house" (he gave him the name of the house) "offer to sell the statue for ten dollars. "

So off they went. The artist made the statue. Then he went out to peddle it. Nobody wanted to buy the statue for seventy-five dollars. But when he got to that house, he said to them, "If you want to buy the statue, I'll let you have it for ten dollars."

The woman said, "If I had money, I'd buy it."

The girl who had killed the thieves said, "I'd buy it if I thought your father wouldn't say anything."

The woman replied, "He won't say anything."

The girl staying at their house bought the statue and they put it in the kitchen. When the man of the house got home, the girl said, "You can say what you want, but I bought the statue of the Virgin Mary."

It was so heavy, they had to hire three or four men to move it. They didn't know the thief was hiding inside the statue.

She said to the man of the house, "We didn't want to put the statue away until you got here and told us where to put it."

"Well," he said, "you're the one who bought the statue, have it placed where you want it. I'd say the best place for the statue of the Virgin is in your bedroom."

As it turned out, the girl was the wife of the thief who was inside the statue.[2]

So be it: they had the three men place the statue in the girl's bedroom—the girl who had killed the thirteen thieves.

The man of the house also had a little baby. His wife had died and his daughter took care of the baby. The baby always wanted to see everything. The man said, "Go show him the statue of the Virgin Mary and see what he does."

When the baby saw the statue, he turned his face away from it, not wanting to see it. He started crying and couldn't stop. They thought this was rather odd, and the man said, "Show him another statue." When they showed him another statue, he was excited and wanted to see it. They showed him the statue of the Virgin Mary again and the same response: he was crying and didn't want to see it.

The man said, "There's some kind of treachery in the statue. We need to see what it is." He went to get his axe and said, "It's just a piece of wood, it's not the real Virgin Mary. I'm going to cut its head off."

He chopped off the statue's head, and there was blood coming out. They discovered the fourteenth thief, the one who had the top of his head cut off, hidden in the statue.

The thief was actually the girl's husband. She had married him. Now the man of the house had chopped off the head of the thief, so both he and the girl were widows. So they got married.

The girl's parents always believed that at any minute she'd be back to get her belongings. She wasn't coming. One day out of the blue, she showed up with her husband.

Her father said, "This is not the man you married."

She said, "No! You made me marry the thief, as I said I'd never say no to anything you'd ask of me. I killed thirteen thieves, cut off the top of the head of the fourteenth thief, my husband. Then he hid himself in a statue of the Virgin Mary which we bought, and it was in the house where I was staying. The man of the house chopped off his head. Now all fourteen thieves are dead!"

Her father said, "You did a good thing. You killed thirteen thieves with your sword and the fourteenth was also destroyed."

So they returned to their house. I wrote them a letter but they never answered.

12. The Boy Who Was Good Company

L'Enfant-de-la-bonne-compagnie

Very widespread in Acadia, where more than ten versions have been collected, this tale[1] of Type 885**, *The Foster Children*, is very rare elsewhere in the world; Aarne and Thompson have only picked up four versions on the border of Finland and Sweden.[2] However, in the Acadian versions, the adopted children give up their place to two schoolchildren—the daughter of a king and a boy found adrift on a river.[3] This narrative develops the theme of faithfulness in friendship which can help in confronting all obstacles: the weather, the parents, the distances.

The Boy Who Was Good Company

THE BOY WHO WAS GOOD COMPANY is a story about a King and Queen who had been married for eight years and had no children. Shortly thereafter, the Queen had a baby girl. When the baby was three months old, the King asked the Queen, "How would you like to go for a ride by horse and buggy up along the river?"

"Ah!" the Queen replied, "I'd love to go."

So off they went. They had gone quite a way

along the river when they suddenly heard the sound of a child crying. They noticed a small box floating with the river's current, coming towards the shore. The King said to his wife, "I think the crying is coming from the box."

The King got down from the wagon, picked up the small box, opened it, and discovered a little boy. They thought he was about three months old. They said, "It's a tramp who had this baby and, to get rid of it, she decided to let him drown."

The baby had not swallowed any water yet. The King asked the Queen, "What are we going to do?"

"Well," she replied, "if you agree, we're going to bring him to our castle and raise him. He would be good company for our little girl and they could go to school together."

"But," he said, "what are we going to call him?"

"Well, we're going to name him The Boy Who Was Good Company."

Well, that was fine.

When the children were old enough to go to school together, they went arm-in-arm and they came home arm-in-arm. But when they reached the age of fifteen or sixteen, they made the most of each other; and the King said to the Queen, "Do you know what's going to happen to us? The Boy Who Was Good Company, whom we found along the shore of the river, when he'll be old enough he'll marry our daughter, and that will be a disgrace for us. She'll be married to a little bastard that we found along the river. He has to die."

"Well," the Queen replied, "it's not my child, so do what you want with him."

The next morning the King said to his daughter, "Tell your teacher today to come and see me after school, I want to speak to him."

Sure enough, she told the teacher. At four in the afternoon the teacher arrived; the daughter saw him coming and snuck into her father's sitting room and hid behind the desk. Suddenly the teacher entered the room and said to the King, "You asked for me?"

The King said, "Yes." The King then reached into his pocket and took out a small bottle of poison and said, "Tomorrow during recess, you'll have all the children go outside but keep The Boy Who Was Good Company in the school. You'll explain that you want to give him extra lessons because he's so smart. Make him swallow one teaspoon of this stuff. It tastes good, but it's pure poison. He will be dead in five minutes. Send someone to us with news of the death. Everyone will think that he died suddenly and we'll go get him to have him buried."

The daughter overheard this conversation. So the next morning they went to school together. She mentioned nothing, but at recess time the teacher said, "Everyone, go play outside. The Boy Who Was Good Company, you stay inside for a few more lessons."

This was fine but the King's daughter refused

to go out. There was no way of making the boy drink the poison. At four o'clock, the King and Queen saw both their daughter and The Boy Who Was Good Company walking home from school. The King said to his wife, "How come he wasn't able to make him take the poison?"

During the night when everyone was in bed, the daughter got up and wrote a letter which said, "Remember that I promised to marry you when I would be old enough for us to get married." She had a little red handkerchief on which she wrote in one corner her name and in the other corner the name of The Boy Who Was Good Company. On their way to school the next day, she said, "How did you feel yesterday when I wouldn't obey the teacher?"

"Oh, yes," he said, "I found that tough. I thought you were a good little girl but you did disobey the teacher."

"But," she said, "if I had gone outside instead of staying in school, you would have been carried off to be buried. Papa gave a bottle of poison to the teacher to make you swallow; that's why I didn't want to leave the school."

"My God!" the boy replied, "I've never caused any trouble to either your mother or father. Why would they want to poison me?"

"Well," she said, "you have reached the age of sixteen. You are very smart, you're big and strong, you can make a life for yourself. If need be, they will destroy you sooner or later."

The girl gave him the letter she had written;

he put it in his pocket and left. He went to the city and saw a big steamboat at the wharf. He went to the wharf and the captain noticed the boy. The captain asked him, "Could we hire you? Our cook quit and we need another one."

"Well," the boy said, "I've never cooked before but if you have a cookbook, I can follow it."

"We have one."

The boy was hired and they went aboard the boat. They sailed out to sea only to encounter stormy weather. Fog and storm—they could see nothing at all. The storm lasted close to five days. They were lost at sea, but the captain explained, "If the sun could appear, that I could take the sun" [that is, use the sextant] "I could find the direction." All of a sudden the sunlight beamed at exactly noon. The Boy Who Was Good Company had bought sea gear before setting out on this trip. He took the sun, but the captain didn't have time to take it before the sun disappeared behind the clouds. The mate noticed and told the captain, "I believe that The Boy Who Was Good Company has taken the sun. Let's go see."

They asked the boy, "Did you take the sun?"

"Yes."

"Show it to us."

Sure enough, he had taken [a reading of] the sun. It was now around midnight. They were still lost. The boy said to the captain, "You are going the opposite direction from your destination. Put your steamboat towards the north and within two hours, if you're still lost, I'll burn all my marine gear."

The captain replied, "Well, I'm lost, so I may as well follow your advice."

The captain turned the boat towards the north; within one hour a red light appeared. The captain said, "I know where we are now. We're not lost anymore."

He said to his mate, "The Boy Who Was Good Company is too smart to be a cook. He'll be my mate and you'll be my second mate and then the second mate will be the cook...." The captain said, "That's that."

When they returned to their country, when the steamboat was unloaded, the captain informed The Boy Who Was Good Company, "I'll give you my steamboat. I've made lots of money for the company that runs this operation. They gave me the boat and said, when I'm tired of navigating, to give the boat to my mate. At the present time, you're my mate. You'll take over this boat!"

So now the boy was captain of the steamboat. Once out to sea, The Boy Who Was Good Company went to his cabin to look in his trunk. He found the letter that the King's daughter had given to him before he left home. He had never opened the letter. He opened the letter only to discover the message, "Remember, we promised each other marriage when we're old enough to get married." There was also one hundred dollars and the red silk handkerchief with their names written on it. He had left when he was sixteen years old; he was now thirty-two years old. He went up on deck and told his mate, "Change course."

He showed his mate which country he needed to reach. The mate thought that this sudden change of route was strange but he had to listen to the captain. When they arrived at their destination, which was where the King and Queen lived, he found the King's castle with a nice white bench in front; the King's daughter was sitting there, but also another man, and next to them the King and Queen. They didn't recognize him at all. He was dressed as a captain, big and grand. He eventually met a fellow on the road that he recognized from when they went to school together. His friend told him, "The King's daughter is getting married tomorrow!"

"Ah!" he said, "the King's daughter is getting married tomorrow?"

"Yes."

The Boy Who Was Good Company returned to see the King's home. They still didn't know him. When he passed by the daughter, he took out his red silk pocket handkerchief and pretended to drop it right at the girl's feet. She picked it up and noticed right away the names she had written in each corner. She recognized the handkerchief....

She asked her parents, "May I go to my room with the captain? I'd like to speak to him for a minute."

"Ah," they replied, "yes, sure."

When she got to the room, she asked, "Is it possible that you are The Boy Who Was Good Company that Papa kept for sixteen years?"

The captain replied, "Yes, it's me. And you're on the verge of getting married tomorrow after our promise to each other to wait until we're old enough to marry."

"Well," she said, "you've been gone sixteen years and I've heard no news from you."

"Well," he said, "if you still want to marry me, there's still time. What time are you getting married tomorrow?"

"At ten o'clock."

"Well," he said, "at nine o'clock I'm going to come here with my mate and his wife who's aboard the steamboat. They can be our best man and maid of honour. I'm going to approach your father and your fiancé to invite them to visit my boat and see the town from it. We'll then sneak off to the church and be married."

"Ah," she said, "yes."

Sure enough, the next morning the King and the fiancé went to visit the boat. The fiancé said, "We'll return by nine-thirty because we're getting married at ten."

The priest married The Boy Who Was Good Company and the King's daughter. He gave the couple their marriage certificate, and when they got to the King's castle, The Boy Who Was Good Company said, "Here, look at this, the other guy won't get her—I've got her."

"Ah!" the King said, "I'll call the police, I'll have you arrested. I thought more of you than this, a captain of a big steamboat, coming here and stealing my daughter."

"Ah," he said to the King, "it's not me who's going to get caught, you're going to be arrested. Do you remember raising a child named The Boy Who Was Good Company for sixteen years?"

The King said, "Yes."

"Well," he said, "that's me, here in front of you today. You gave a bottle of poison to my teacher to get rid of me, but your daughter saved my life. Now I have her as my wife. It is I who's going to have the police take you away for giving that bottle of poison."

The King dropped to his knees and begged for forgiveness and promised the captain half of his fortune.

The captain said, "No, all I want from you is your daughter."

Then he took his wife and they climbed aboard the steamboat.

I was on the wharf waving good-bye.

13. The Seven-Headed Beast

La Bête à sept têtes

This tale, *The Dragon-Slayer*, is of Type 300 and is one of the most widespread in French Canada. More than one hundred versions have been collected,[1] of which fifteen versions were found in Acadia. Marcellin Haché[2] relates a version, a remarkable summary.

A mother prefers her two oldest sons to her youngest. Feeling neglected, he goes off hunting into the forest (I). He arrives at a log cabin, inhabited by the King's daughter who'd been kidnapped by three thieves. The boy decides to save her. He then comes upon a second log cabin, where he meets the King's second daughter who's been kidnapped by two thieves. He arrives in a city that's in mourning and finds out that it's because the King's two daughters have been kidnapped and the third daughter will soon be eaten by a seven-headed beast (IIa, b; IIIb). The boy confronts the beast and with his first arrow cuts off six of the heads, and with the second arrow cuts off the seventh head of the beast (IV).

To prove his feat, he cuts out the seven tongues of the beast, puts them in his pocket and leaves (Va; VIa). After the boy leaves, another guy comes along and threatens the King's daughter into agreeing to marry him (Vb; VIe). He brings the seven heads as proof to the King that he killed the beast. At the moment he's showing the King the seven heads, the hero displays the seven tongues (VIIa, c). The antagonist is sent home without punishment. The boy goes to get the two girls, his mother and his two brothers to celebrate a triple wedding.

The Seven-Headed Beast

THE STORY OF THE SEVEN-HEADED BEAST is about a widow that had three sons. One night, she said to her two eldest sons, "Tomorrow morning, we're going to the city."

The next morning while they were getting ready to go into the city, the third son, the youngest, said, "Mother, I'm going too."

His mother replied, "I don't want you to come because you'll just cause trouble for us, maybe even have us put in prison."

The youngest didn't listen to her. He waited until his mother and brothers were gone. When he figured they'd been gone long enough, he left, following far behind. He had an arrow, and there was nothing he couldn't kill with his arrow. He followed the road his mother and brothers had taken, but after a while he went into the woods to try and kill some type of bird or anything else, but to no avail— he found nothing. He went further into the woods, and all of a sudden it was dark. Evening had come.

114

He was lost in the woods. He hollered. Not a word. Nothing. Well, he spent the night in the woods. The next morning he walked, but instead of walking towards the road he was going the opposite way. Soon he found a cabin of wood, of branches. He entered the cabin and saw a very thin girl with almost no clothing on her body. He asked the girl, "Why are you here?"

"Well," she said, "I was captured by three thieves in my father's garden. I am the King's daughter. They brought me here and feed me what they can catch."

"Well," he said, "I'm here to save your life."

"You're counting on saving my life? But," she said, "they're going to kill you."

"Oh no," he said, "I'm going to hide."

She begged him to take her with him. He said, "I can't take you with me. I'm lost and don't know where we are. You will not die here. I will come and get you."

So be it. He bid her good-bye and left. He walked for quite a while and again came upon a girl in a log cabin. He entered and asked her, "What are you doing here?"

"Well," she said, "I am a daughter of the King of Paris who's been captured by two thieves, and they dumped me here."

She was insistent that he take her with him, but he said, "I cannot take you with me, I'm lost. You will not die here. I'll come and get you when I find out where we are."

Anyway, around three o'clock in the afternoon, he found himself in the city, lost. Good! He had heard that in the city, there was always music, pianos, red flags, etc—lots of commotion. Today, you could have heard a mouse run. A black flag was flying at half mast. He thought this was very strange. He approached a man on the street and asked, "Why is the city in a state of mourning?"

"Well," he said, "you know that the King has three daughters. Two were captured by thieves, and tomorrow morning at ten o'clock his third daughter must be eaten by The Seven-Headed Beast."

"But," he said, "why is that? Why is the King's daughter to be eaten by The Seven-Headed Beast?"

"Well," he said, "there's been a law passed that every year a girl has to be eaten by The Seven-Headed Beast. They put numbers on cards matching the number of girls, put them in a box, and the girl who's unlucky enough to have her number picked will have to be eaten by The Seven-Headed Beast. This year it's the King's daughter whose number was picked. There's no other way—she has to be eaten."

"Is that so?" the widow's son said. "Well, if I knew where The Seven-Headed Beast was, I guarantee you I'd kill it."

"Ah!" he said, "the King hired thousands of soldiers, the best warriors, and they couldn't kill it."

The widow's son took off with his arrow. Another man went to show him where the King's daughter was. She was tied to a tree in the forest. She said, "You poor thing, get out of here. The Seven-Headed Beast will be here in five minutes, and instead of eating one he'll eat two."

The widow's son said, "Let him come!"

All of a sudden, he saw it coming. The beast went for the girl, then for him. With the first stroke of his arrow he cut off six of its heads. There was only one head remaining. It backed off. The beast went away, but all of a sudden it came back, chasing the girl. The widow's son was right in front of the girl. With the second stroke of his arrow he cut off the seventh head. He said to the girl, "The Seven-Headed Beast is dead. In the future, there will be no more girls eaten by The Seven-Headed Beast."

The King's daughter said, "No. I'm happy for myself as well as all the other girls. But," she said, "what proof will you take to Papa that you have killed The Seven-Headed Beast?"

He cut out the seven tongues, put them in a bag and then put them in his pocket. Meanwhile, the man who had shown him to the King's daughter was hiding in the woods, watching all this. When the widow's son was gone, he went to see the King's daughter and said, "You must tell your father that I killed The Seven-Headed Beast. That way, I can have your hand in marriage and half your father's fortune."

"Oh," she replied, "I cannot do that!"

"Well," he said, "if you won't do it, perhaps The Seven-Headed Beast did not kill you but I will."

My God! She was stuck. She was forced into saying that she would marry him. Well, when they arrived at the castle the King asked, "What proof do you have that you killed The Seven-Headed Beast?"

The man replied, "I brought the seven heads."

"Show them to me."

The King recognized the seven heads. While he was examining the heads, the widow's son arrived with the seven tongues. He said to the King, "Have you ever seen beasts with heads but no tongues?"

Ah! The King answered, "No creature has a head but no tongue."

The widow's son said, "Why don't you open the mouths of the seven heads?"

The King opened the seven mouths and found that all the tongues had been cut out.

The widow's son put his hand deep into his pocket and said, "Here, Mister King. It's not him that killed The Seven-Headed Beast, it is I. And here are the seven tongues."

The King asked his daughter, "Why did you tell me such a lie?"

The King's daughter replied, "Well, this man came to me and said if I didn't say that it was him who killed The Seven-Headed Beast—so that he could get my hand in marriage and half your fortune—he would take my life."

"Ah! Ah! Well," he said, "so that's the kind of man you are."

He then asked the widow's son, "Give me a punishment for this man, I'm going to punish him."

The widow's son replied, "Well, in any case, he didn't kill her. Just send him home, that's all I want."

"That's fine."

The King was a widow and so was the boy's mother. The King married the boy's mother and her three sons married the King's three daughters. They celebrated their weddings all together. I was there, at the wedding.

14. The Princess with Golden Hair

La Princesse aux cheveux d'or

This tale[1] is particularly elaborate and is similar to two other tales, Type 312, *The Giant-killer and his Dog (Bluebeard)*, and Type 531, *Ferdinand the True and Ferdinand the False*, which have in common a horse that talks, derived from Type 551, *The Sons on a Quest for a Wonderful Remedy for their Father*, the Fountain of Youth. It is especially widespread throughout Europe, India, Indonesia, the two Americas and even Africa.

With the assistance of his little horse that talks, P'tit Jean is able to accomplish incredible feats ordered under threat of death by the King, who will stop at nothing to get The Princess with Golden Hair to marry him. Contrary to other tales, here the exploits of P'tit Jean are not for his benefit. It is only at the end of the story he ends up marrying The Princess with Golden Hair.

Gérald E. Aucoin published a version[2] of this tale collected from the same Marcellin Haché in December of 1957, which includes two extra components. When the hero flees, he is obliged to eat something in order to survive, and when he is the King's gardener he must destroy the garden in order to sow again. These are optional segments which are not essential for the flow of the story.

In this tale, the reason for the lock of golden hair that P'tit Jean has to wear and needs to keep hidden, is quite vague.

The Princess with Golden Hair

THIS IS A STORY ABOUT A WIDOW who had a son named P'tit Jean. One morning he said to his mother, "I have to leave with my gun and try to make a living."

On the road that he took, he found nothing to kill. He could see woods farther on and thought perhaps there was something over there. He walked past a castle and when he reached the other side of the fence, someone called him. He turned towards the castle and saw a Negro, the blackest man he'd ever seen. The Negro said, "Come here, you!"

P'tit Jean didn't respond and all of a sudden a big black dog arrived in front of him. He untied his bag and gave the dog a piece of bread. The dog didn't do him any harm. The Negro hollered, "Come here!"

The Negro asked him, "What are you looking for with your gun?"

P'tit Jean replied, "I'm looking for work."

"Is that so?" the Negro said. "Well, I'll hire you. You'll sleep here tonight. Tomorrow morning, I'm going to go work on my farm while you stay at the castle making the beds and cooking. I will be here for lunch at exactly noon. Not at eleven-thirty or a quarter after twelve but at noon. My lunch has to be ready!"

"I understand," P'tit Jean said. "It'll be done."

"You can cook anything you want."

The next morning before leaving, the Negro gave him the keys to the rooms, all fourteen of them, and said, "Here's key number fourteen. There's number one, two, three, four up to fourteen. I order you not to open door fourteen. You can open it if you want, but watch yourself if you do. I'm giving you the key anyway."

The Negro went to work on the farm and the widow's son was in the castle. He made lunch and unlocked all the rooms until he got to room fourteen. He hesitated before inserting the key to unlock the door. The Negro had told him, "Misfortune to anyone who opens the door." Anyway, he inserted the key in the lock but then got very afraid and removed it. At eleven-thirty, the Negro arrived at the castle.

"It's strange, you told me you'd be back at noon. Lunch is not ready."

"Ah! Ah!" the Negro said. "P'tit Jean, my poor fellow. You have put the key in the lock to open the door."

P'tit Jean said, "No."

The Negro said, "Even if I was two hundred miles from here, I'd know if you put the key in the lock. I just know. Well, I gave you the key, you can open it if you want, but misfortune to you if you do."

They had lunch. The next morning the Negro went to work on the farm and P'tit Jean stayed at the castle. It was around ten o'clock and he said, "It's all a bluff, I'm opening that door." He inserted the key in the lock, opened the door, and what came face to face with him? A small black horse in the room. The little horse said, "P'tit Jean, you poor thing, you opened the door. We have but a quarter of an hour left to live. The Negro knows. The minute you put the key in the lock, he knows. He's going to come here and take our lives. Do you see the lock of golden hair on the window over there?"

P'tit Jean answered, "Yes."

The horse said, "Well, put it on your head." (There was also the bladder of a pig that was all bloated up, it was really big.) "Cut it open and put it over the hair. Don't show the lock of golden hair to anyone because if you do, misfortune to you. Do you see the saddle over there? Put it on my back and we'll leave."

They had time to do this before the Negro returned. When he arrived, he went into room fourteen. The little black horse was gone and so was P'tit Jean. He had missed them.

All right! P'tit Jean kept on going on the little black horse. That night, they arrived in the city. He put the little black horse in a barn and went to seek out the King to ask for lodging for the night. The King said, "Yes, you can sleep here."

Well, the Queen had died, so the next morning they had to go to the funeral. When it was all over, they had breakfast at the castle and the King said to P'tit Jean, "If you were a gardener, I would hire you. My gardener left us."

"Oh!" P'tit Jean said, "that's my first profession."

He had never done this before but he managed to get hired. The King was reading the newspaper which said that a princess with golden hair existed in the world. It didn't mention where she was. He said to P'tit Jean, "You must go get me The Princess with Golden Hair."

"With pleasure, if you want to tell me where she is."

"Well," he said, "it says in the newspaper that there's one, but it doesn't say where she is. I give you three days, and if at the end of the three days you don't have The Princess with Golden Hair here, I will kill you beside my castle."

P'tit Jean said, "I have to go get my little horse."

He went to consult his little horse, his little black horse who said to P'tit Jean, "Do you see the trouble you're in? Go see the King and tell him to give you his largest frigate, all loaded with red silk. Go two hundred miles from here and give it all away for nothing. Maybe The Princess with Golden Hair will go there to obtain a piece, and when she's aboard, just sail off and come back."

Sure enough, off he went with a full load of red silk, all for nothing. When the princess came aboard to get a piece of silk, P'tit Jean said to the captain, "Sail off as fast as you can."

That steamboat went forty miles an hour. When the princess got up to leave, she lost sight of land. She was very angry with P'tit Jean. In a rage, she threw her keys in the ocean. He said, "Well, in order to save my life, I have to take you to my country."

When they arrived, the King asked the princess, "Are you going to marry me now?"

She replied, "I cannot marry you until my castle is here."

The King went looking for P'tit Jean and said, "You have to go and get the castle that belongs to The Princess with Golden Hair."

He went to see his little black horse and said, "The King wants me to get the castle that belongs to The Princess with Golden Hair."

"Well," he said, "go see the King and tell him to give you the same ship loaded with rum, and then go. There are four giants that take care of The Princess with Golden Hair. They're strong enough to take each corner of the castle and move it."

All right. He went to see the King and said, "I want you to give me the same frigate loaded up with rum so I can get the castle that belongs to The Princess with Golden Hair."

The King said, "All right then, go!"

He went over there and found the four giants. He gave them a ton of rum. They drank it all and said, "Ah! if there was more."

P'tit Jean replied, "Well, if you get the castle

that belongs to The Princess with Golden Hair and put it on the back of my ship, I will give you another ton of rum."

They put the castle on the back of the ship. P'tit Jean left to come home. When he got to the castle, the King asked, "Did you bring the castle that belongs to The Princess with Golden Hair?"

"Yes," he said, "it's on the back of the ship. Hire some people and have it placed where she wants it."

The King hired some people and had the castle moved where she wanted it. He then asked the princess, "Now, will you marry me?"

When the princess arrived at the door of her castle, she had no keys. She said, "I will not marry you unless I have the keys to my castle."

The King returned to see P'tit Jean and said, "You have to get the keys that belong to The Princess with Golden Hair."

P'tit Jean replied, "What you have asked me to do until now was possible—to get the girl, The Princess with Golden Hair, to get the castle—but the keys that belong to the princess? I myself saw her throw her keys into the ocean, where there might have been four thousand feet of water. Who's going to get the keys at the bottom?"

The King wouldn't hear of this. P'tit Jean went to see his little black horse and told him the story.

"Ah!" the little horse said. "You showed your lock of golden hair to someone?"

P'tit Jean said, "No."

"Someone saw it and they told the King, because otherwise he wouldn't ask you to do something like this. Tell the King to give you the same frigate with a fishing crew. Do you know approximately where she threw away the keys?"

"Ah," he answered, "yes."

He then said, "Maybe you could catch some fish that would have the keys that belong to the princess."

The crew fished until four o'clock. There were plenty of fish, but no keys. Around a quarter to five, they threw another line and caught a big cod fish. They cut it up and the keys that belonged to The Princess with Golden Hair were inside the fish. P'tit Jean was happy. He returned to the castle on the third day and gave the keys to the King. The King gave the keys to the princess with the golden hair and asked, "Will you marry me now that you have your keys?"

She replied, "Well, you know that you have reached the age of seventy-five, and that I'm just a young seventeen-year-old girl. I see in the newspaper that there's a Fountain of Youth somewhere in the world, but it doesn't say where. If you could find that water and become twenty-five again, then I'd marry you."

The King returned to see P'tit Jean who was in the garden, and explained this to him. P'tit Jean said, "If you could tell me where it is, it wouldn't be difficult, but it doesn't say where it is."

P'tit Jean went to see his little horse and told him all this. The little horse said, "Do you see, P'tit Jean, the trouble you're in? The Fountain of Youth is two hundred miles from here in a small lake on a big mountain. The only way to get there is by a trail about four feet wide and it's full of beasts—lions, wolves, bears—all sorts of ferocious beasts. You'll probably be devoured, but in any case, it's no worse being eaten by beasts in the forest than to be killed by the king."

P'tit Jean saddled up the little horse with the same gear taken from the Negro's castle and they left. They crossed through without any harm coming to them and filled up his bottle with water from the Fountain of Youth. They returned, passing through the forest without difficulty. He gave the water to the King, who put the bottle on his bedroom window.

The King had a servant in the castle. She entered the bedroom to make the bed and do the dusting. Inadvertently, she knocked down the bottle, spilling the contents. She went to get a rag to wipe the mess she'd made on the floor. Then she saw a jug under the bed. She took the jug and filled up the bottle. She put the bottle back where it was with a glass next to it. She had time to do this before the King entered the bedroom. The King entered, saw the bottle and the glass. On the bottle it read, "Drink one glass: a full water glass without tasting it." He drank a full glass, and within five minutes the King was dead. It was pure poison that was in the bottle. The King's daughter happened to enter her father's bedroom where she found her father dead on the floor, black as the stove. She cried out to the servant, "My father's been poisoned, dead on the floor."

The servant said, "It's not me who did this. I just took the bottle and filled it up with what was in the jug under your father's bed."

The King's daughter said, "This is pure poison. It's pure poison that was in the bottle."

They buried the King. P'tit Jean ended up marrying The Princess with Golden Hair.

I had my eye on the King's daughter but couldn't have her.

15. The Bird of Truth
L'Oiseau de vérité

This tale,[1] of Type 550, *Search for the Golden Bird*, unfolds in an elaborate way which relates to components of Types 301A (*Quest for a Vanished Princess*), 329 (*Hiding from the Devil*) and 313 (*The Girl as Helper in the Hero's Flight*). It is especially widespread in Europe, the Orient, Asia and America.[2]

In this wonderful and fantastic tale, The Bird of Truth steals golden apples from the King's orchard. During his pursuit, P'tit Jean goes down into a hole where he discovers an extraordinary castle, outsmarts the plans of a witch, fights ferocious beasts, frees three girls, meets up with a King who makes him undergo great trials in order to win his daughter's hand in marriage.... Thanks to the advice of the little black horse that he obtained from the witch, he is able to undergo these tests successfully and marry the princess. He also finds The Bird of Truth and relieves his little horse of a spell, so that the horse becomes a man again.

The end of this tale as Father Anselme Chiasson collected it, and of the version collected from the same storyteller by Gérald E. Aucoin,[3] leaves a lot to be desired. With Mr. Aucoin's permission, we are able to present a more authentic and logical ending, combining his version, Father Anselme's, and memories recalled during Father Anselme's adolescence.

The Bird of Truth

THE BIRD OF TRUTH is a story about a King who had three sons. He also had a garden that produced golden apples, and noticed that one was stolen every night. He said to his oldest son, "If you spend the night in the garden and tell me tomorrow morning who steals my apple, I'll give you half my fortune."

The King's oldest son replied, "I'm going to go."

Sure enough, he went. The King had a bench made so he could sit down and rest. His son walked until ten o'clock, sat on the bench and fell asleep. The apple was always stolen at midnight. The thief would steal the apple at exactly midnight. The next morning, the King went into the garden, counted his apples—there was one missing. He said to his son, "Ah! The apple was stolen, did you recognize the thief?"

"No! I didn't see anything. I sat on the bench and fell asleep."

Well, the one stealing the apple was The Bird of Truth. The bird had noticed that the King had placed a bench in the garden. He cast a spell upon the bench, that any man who sat on the bench would fall asleep. Nobody knew about this.

The second son said, "Papa, I'm going to go. I guarantee you, I will not fall asleep."

The second son went to the garden. There, he

walked until about ten o'clock, sat on the bench and fell asleep. At midnight the apple was stolen. The next morning, the King went to the garden, counted the apples and there was still one missing. The third son, P'tit Jean, said to his father, "I'm going to go tonight. I guarantee you, I will not fall asleep."

P'tit Jean did the same. Around eleven o'clock, he sat on the bench and thought to himself, "I'm going to fall asleep." He got up from the bench. At midnight, who arrives to steal the apple? The Bird of Truth. He aimed his pistol at the bird but missed. The Bird of Truth flew towards a big black mountain. P'tit Jean noted the direction in which the bird flew, and left. The next morning, the King counted his apples, and once again there was one missing.

The King asked P'tit Jean, "You were not able to kill him?"

"No. He flew up on a big black mountain. I grabbed him, plucked out a few feathers, but couldn't hold on to him.'

"Ah!" the King said, "we're going to go see where he went."

They took off. From time to time, they'd find a feather, one here, one there. They followed the direction of the feathers. All of a sudden, they came upon a hole. They couldn't see the bottom of the hole. It was maybe two hundred feet deep. The King said, "I'm going to get some rope and a basket. We're going to tie the rope on the basket and you're going to get in the basket. We're going to slide the basket down to the bottom. That way you can see what's at the bottom of the hole."

They put the King's oldest son in the basket and he went down. They had also installed a bell on the rope in case he was in any danger. The oldest son went down into the hole but once he lost sight of the others, he got very scared and rang the bell. They brought him up. The second son went down about fifty feet further but also got scared and came up. P'tit Jean said, "You're all fearful. I guarantee you, I'll go to the bottom."

P'tit Jean got into the basket and went down. All of a sudden, there was slack on the rope. They said, "P'tit Jean is at the bottom." It was dark as hell down there. P'tit Jean felt his way with his hands along the wall, finding a doorknob. He opened the door and found an electric light and a beautiful big staircase. Every twenty feet, there was a light. All of a sudden, he found a castle, a castle underneath the ground, a thousand times more beautiful than his father's castle. He'd never seen anything like it!

He knocked on the door of the castle and heard, "Come in." There was a old woman there. The woman asked, "Why are you here? I've been here for forty years and you're the first man to enter the castle."

"Ah," P'tit Jean said, "I was on my way to see the big cities and I ended up here."

She said, "To get to the big cities, you have to fight at exactly midnight."

"But who do I have to fight?"

She answered, "You'll know when the time comes."

He asked, "How do you expect me to fight? I don't even have a pocket knife to defend myself."

"Well," she said, "come with me."

She guided P'tit Jean into one of the rooms in the castle, where there was a post in the middle of the room surrounded by weapons such as guns, swords, all sorts of things.

She said, "That one is all rusted, an old sword, don't take it. It's good for nothing."

The old woman left P'tit Jean alone in the room. He said to himself, "She told me not to take the rusted sword; I'm going to take it." He took the rusted sword and went upstairs. The woman had told him he'd have to fight at exactly midnight. At midnight, who came to fight P'tit Jean? A lion. A lion who, on his hind legs, stood twice the height of P'tit Jean. The lion said, "The two of us are going to fight."

"Yes," P'tit Jean answered, "I'm going to try."

At the first strike of the sword, P'tit Jean cut off the lion's head. All the power was in the rusted sword, but he didn't know this. The old woman thought he was going to pick another weapon but he took the right weapon without knowing. P'tit Jean went to see the old woman and said, "I killed the lion."

"What? You killed the lion?"

"Yes."

"Well," she said, "come with me."

She guided him to another room, in which there was a beautiful girl. She said to P'tit Jean, "The girl belongs to you. She belonged to the lion and now she's yours."

"Good!" P'tit Jean said. "Papa is a widow, it'll be a girl for him."

The next evening, the old woman said, "You have to fight again for the second night."

That night, who arrived to fight him? The seven-headed beast. The beast attacked in an attempt to devour P'tit Jean, but at the first strike with his sword, he removed all seven heads. He entered the castle and said to the old woman, "I've killed the seven-headed beast."

She replied, "What? You killed the seven-headed beast!"

She guided P'tit Jean into another room, where there was a girl, even more beautiful than the other one. P'tit Jean said, "This will be a girl for my brother. I'm getting rid of her."

On the third night, the old woman said, "You have to fight again for the last time."

On the third night, it was a unicorn that came to fight him. He tried to charge at P'tit Jean's body with his horn. He braced himself against the castle. The unicorn tried to charge at him but to no avail. P'tit Jean struck the unicorn with his sword, and at the first blow, he cut off the unicorn's head. He said to the old woman, "I cut off the unicorn's head."

"Good!" she said. "Come with me." She guided

him to another room, where again there was a girl, even more beautiful than the other two.

"Well," P'tit Jean said, "this will be a girl for my second brother. Now, I'm going to go see the big cities."

The old woman said, "Go to the barn. I have three horses from which you can choose. Don't take the little green horse, he's thin and good for nothing. The other two horses, well, the only thing missing is their ability to speak."

P'tit Jean went to the barn. Everything was just as she said. He took the little green horse. He left to go see the big cities. When he arrived at the big city, his little green horse spoke and said, "What are you going to do in a country that you're not familiar with?"

"Well," P'tit Jean answered, "I'm going to go ask the King for a place for the night, for me and my horse."

The King said to him, "Yes. Put your horse in the barn and come to the castle. You'll spend the night with us."

The next morning, P'tit Jean asked for the King's daughter in marriage. The King answered, "For you to have my daughter's hand in marriage, you have to hide for three days. If I find you, you will be hanged outside my castle. If I don't find you, you can have my daughter's hand in marriage."

Well, P'tit Jean went to see his little horse and said, "The King asked me to hide for three days in order to have his daughter's hand in marriage.

Where do I hide? I'm in a country that I know nothing about."

The little horse replied, "Go where the fence is over there. There's a pack of ferocious beasts. You'll hide there."

The next morning, the King searched everywhere but found nothing. At seven o'clock, the bell rang. This was P'tit Jean's cue to come home. The King said to P'tit Jean, "I wasn't able to find you."

P'tit Jean said, "That's your fault, not mine."

The King said, "I'll try again tomorrow morning."

The second morning, P'tit Jean asked his little horse, "Where am I going to go hide?"

The little horse answered, "Well, look into my mouth. There's a loose tooth: pull it out and hide there."

P'tit Jean pulled out the tooth and hid there. The King searched everywhere but couldn't find P'tit Jean. At the end of the day, the King said, "I missed you again this morning."

P'tit Jean said, "Well, that's your fault, not mine."

The third day, P'tit Jean hid himself in the left ear of the little horse, and the King couldn't find him.

The King then said, "I'm going to go hide for three mornings. If you don't find me, you will be hanged outside my castle. If you find me, you will have my daughter's hand in marriage."

The first morning, P'tit Jean said to his little

horse, "Where could the King be hiding?"

His little horse replied, "The King is hidden in his garden. He is hidden under the soil at the end of the garden."

P'tit Jean went to the garden and found the King.

The second morning, his little green horse said, "The King is hidden in a large potato. Split the potato in two and the King will come out."

The third morning, his little green horse said, "The King is hidden in the small lake in his garden. He's turned into a fish. The minute you put a line into the lake, he's going to bite, and as soon as he's out of the water, he'll turn into a man again."

P'tit Jean went over there. The King's daughter said, "P'tit Jean, find my father. He's going to kill you—there's only five minutes before seven o'clock."

P'tit Jean said, "Ah well, I'm going to throw a fishing line in the lake."

The King's daughter said, "It's no use, there's never been any fish in this small lake."

P'tit Jean knew. It was the little horse who'd told him. He said, "In any case, I'm going to throw a line."

He threw the line into the water. The fish took the bait. When the fish was out of the water, the King tumbled at his feet.

The King said, "Ah, you found me."

P'tit Jean asked the King, "Are you going to give me your daughter's hand in marriage?"

The King replied, "Yes. I promised. I give her to you. But you must live with me here in my castle beneath the ground."4

P'tit Jean and the King's daughter got married and went to bed on the third floor. The King's daughter asked P'tit Jean, "Do you know who steals the golden apples from your father?"

P'tit Jean answered, "Yes, it's a bird."

She said, "It's The Bird of Truth. He belongs to me. It's me that was sending him to steal your father's golden apples. Now, you are my husband, The Bird of Truth belongs to you. Only you can get him to speak."

She had The Bird of Truth come to their room.

P'tit Jean didn't want to stay beneath the ground. He asked his little green horse to come underneath their window so they could leave at midnight.

There was a small stove in their room. He lit the stove before midnight. The King's daughter gave him three beans and said, "Put the beans to roast on the stove. They will burst and make noise. While my father hears noise coming from the room, he will believe we're still here."

At midnight, they dropped onto the little green horse, P'tit Jean, the King's daughter and The Bird of Truth. They took off. They returned to the old woman's castle where he'd got his little horse. He put his horse in the barn and as he was walking out of the barn, he noticed a young man.

He thought this was strange. He went to see the old woman and asked, "Is there any other man here?"

The old woman replied, "No. You're the only man I've seen here."

P'tit Jean returned to the barn and still the young man was there. He asked him, "What are you doing here?"

The young man answered, "I acted like you, but I did not choose the rusted sword, and the old woman changed me into a little green horse. You have relieved me and I have become a man again."

P'tit Jean said, "Well, come with me."

He went and rang the bell so that his brothers would haul up the basket. His brothers brought up the three girls and P'tit Jean's wife along with The Bird of Truth. They didn't want to send the basket for P'tit Jean to come up. They returned to their father's castle with the girls, P'tit Jean's wife and The Bird of Truth. They said to their father, "We found these four King's daughters. One is for you, the other two for us, and one is P'tit Jean's wife. We also found The Bird of Truth. He was the one stealing your golden apples."

The King tried to get The Bird of Truth to speak but to no effect. The bird didn't say a word.

P'tit Jean stayed in the hole for three days with the other guy. At the end of the third day, he went to see the old woman and said, "You have to bring us up, out of this hole."

"I'm not capable of doing that," said the old woman. "I am not a bird."

"My wicked witch! You're going to bring us up or I will cut your head off with the rusted sword."

"Oh, damn!" The old woman was stuck. She knew that with the rusted sword he could kill her. She brought them up.

When P'tit Jean got to the top, he returned to his father's castle. His wife hugged him. His father said, "Your brothers found and captured The Bird of Truth that was stealing my golden apples."

P'tit Jean asked The Bird of Truth to speak and tell the truth. The bird said, "P'tit Jean killed a lion, the seven-headed beast and a unicorn to save the three girls. It's him who married the princess over there and found me, not his brothers."

The King wanted to punish P'tit Jean's brothers but P'tit Jean said, "No! Just get married and let's celebrate!"

The wedding lasted eight days and if they're not dead, they're still living.

16. The Beautiful Helen

La Belle Hélène

Even though this tale belongs to Type 706, *The Maiden Without Hands* (as does the tale on page 38), "The Beautiful Helen" told by Marcellin Haché to the folklorist Luc Lacourcière[1] is a totally different tale. The main theme is the only thing they have in common.

Jean, who has become a widow, wants to marry his daughter, The Beautiful Helen. She flees from him. She marries the King's son and has two children. While the King's son was gone to war, the mother-in-law has Beautiful Helen's hand cut off at the wrist, and gives orders to have her and the two children killed. The soldiers leave her alive in the forest. Helen loses her children. Sixteen years later, they all meet on the streets of Paris, but they don't recognize each other. A reception at the Pope's house—he is Helen's uncle—gives them a joyous reunion.

The Beautiful Helen

THE STORY OF BEAUTIFUL HELEN is about a girl from Paris. Her father's name was Jean and her mother was the Pope's sister. When Helen was sixteen years old, her mother passed away.

Eighteen months after Jean's wife died, he

left for two and a half months in search of a woman as beautiful as his late wife. He couldn't find one. When he returned, he said to his daughter, "You're the picture of your mother; I'm going to marry you."

"Papa, how can you marry me? It's not possible."

"I'm going to go see your uncle, the Pope," said her father, "to obtain his permission to marry you. Will you marry me?"

His daughter didn't answer; she didn't say yes, nor did she say no. He went to the Pope with this. The Pope said, "It's impossible, Jean, for me to give you a permit to marry your daughter."

"Well," Jean said, "you know that whenever I've gone to war, I've always won my battles. If you do not give me permission to marry my daughter, I will call in my army and order them to burn the whole city, leaving much bloodshed behind."

The Pope then said, "Well, come see me tomorrow morning and I will tell you what to do."

The next morning, Jean returned. The Pope gave him a letter and said, "Give this to your daughter."

When Jean got home he gave the letter to his daughter. The Pope was asking her to marry her father. Well, she found this very difficult to accept. Jean was concerned that she might run away so he told his servant to lock her up in a room and feed her the best possible food. He also added, "I want her to be as beautiful the day I marry her as she is today. Give her everything she wants."

But one evening, Helen said to the servant, "You should give me a knife."

"No," said the servant.

"I'd rather destroy myself than marry my father," Helen said.

"Well, at midnight, I will unlock the window," the servant said. "You'll go out and do with yourself whatever you want."

All right! At midnight, she went out the window. It was really dark. She went to the coast in order to drown herself. When she got to the coast, she found it was very distressing—for a lucid person to try to drown herself. There was a canoe in the water. She got into the canoe. There were no oars. She just let herself go with the current.

She was at sea for two days. The wind picked up; a big wave pushed the canoe to dry land. She got out. The sand was so soft that she sank in the sand up to here [waist high]. She was stuck there, unable to escape. Well, there was a man, Henri, that was out hunting. He saw this and thought it was a bird. He approached to kill it, but as he got closer he realized it wasn't a bird. He went up to the girl and said, "Why are you here?"

She related her story, about what happened with her father. He took her out of the sand and brought her to his castle. Henri was a warrior. He was in charge of an army in the war, just like Helen's father. When they arrived at the castle, he said to Helen, "I have to return to my post at war. You're going to stay in my castle."

Henri's mother was a widow. She didn't want to see him marry this girl. He was gone to war for six months, and when he returned he married Beautiful Helen. His mother didn't want to hear of it but he married her anyway. Henri said to his mother, "Mind your own business and I will mind my own."

Six months after they were married, Henri had to return to war. Before leaving, he had three stamps made, one for himself, one for his wife and one for his servants. Without these stamps, you could not send letters to the army.

Six months after Henri had gone to war—it made a year that they were married—his wife had two boys, the two most handsome boys that they'd ever seen. One was the picture of his father, the other the picture of his mother.

Henri's mother wrote a letter to her son, informing him that his wife had delivered two Negro boys, the ugliest boys in the world. She wrote asking, "Tell me as soon as possible what to do about this." He wrote to his wife, telling her they could stay alive until his return. Henri's mother took the letter before Helen received it. She tore it up and threw it in the stove. She then wrote another letter as if it was her son writing to Helen, ordering the death of Beautiful Helen and her two children because he wasn't the father of those children.

Henri's mother went to Beautiful Helen and asked her, "Did you receive any news from Henri?"

"No," said The Beautiful Helen.

"No? Well, you're going to receive some today and it's a very sad letter."

"What? Was he killed?"

"No, it's worse than that."

"What is it?"

"He asked to have both you and the children killed."

Beautiful Helen dropped to her knees on the bed, praying with God as her witness that she'd never been with another man but her husband Henri. How could he say that he wasn't the father of her children? One was a picture of his father, the other a picture of his mother.

Henri's mother had two soldiers come and chain up Helen. The letter said that they were to cut off her hand at the wrist and keep it as proof that they'd killed The Beautiful Helen. When they cut off her hand, Beautiful Helen said, "I would like you to take the cut-off hand and put it in a small leather bag around my son's neck."

The doctor went over and embalmed the cut-off hand so it would last for forty years. Helen left with her two children and two soldiers who were going to kill her. After a little while, one of the soldiers turned around and noticed that she was crying and asked, "Why are you crying?"

"I see that you're going to kill us. Not for my sake, but for the sake of my children, I would like you to let us live."

"Well," the soldiers said, "if you promise us that you will never leave the forest, we won't kill you. We're going to put you into exile in the forest."

Helen said, "Yes!"

When Helen went into the woods, she spent two nights with her children, feeding them what she could find. One day, she came upon an island about twelve miles long. Only an old man lived on this island, on the very tip of the island. He lived in a small house and looked after his fur traps. Helen put her two children in a small house she'd made out of wood and branches. She was dying of hunger. She went down to the river and fished for trout until she had enough. She fed herself, and her children would get nourishment from her. When she returned to her cabin, her children were gone. They were too young to be off on their own; they were only a year old. She spent the whole night looking for her children, asking God to bring them back. The next morning, she was no further ahead—she couldn't find them.

As she was all alone, she went down to the coast. She saw a ship anchored close to shore. A man came to get some water. When he saw Helen, he asked, "Why are you here? On this island, there's only an old man and an old woman, who live on the tip of the island. They live about twelve miles from here and trap furs to sell them. There's no other woman but that old woman on this island."

Beautiful Helen replied, "I would like to be transported back to Paris, where I'm from."

"That's just where I'm going," he said.

She went aboard the ship and they left for Paris.

One day, the old man who lived on the tip of the island went hunting. He saw a lion and a wolf fighting. When he advanced to kill them, he noticed two children in the animals' den. He thought to himself, the lion and the wolf are fighting to see who's going to eat the children. He took his gun, killed the lion and the wolf, brought the children home with him and kept them for sixteen years.

He brought them up as Catholics and taught them well. When the children were sixteen—he was rich—he gave them some money and said to them, "On the other side of the island, ships often come to the shore to get water. You could go aboard."

"We're going to go," the children replied.

They went there; a ship was arriving. Once on shore, the captain asked the old man who was there with the children, "Why do you have two children with you? I spoke to you about twelve years ago and you told me you've never had any children. Here you are today with two sixteen-year-olds."

The old man told him the story of how he'd found the children in the lion and the wolf's den. The captain said, "I transported a woman from this island to Paris sixteen years ago."

"Ah well," the old man said, "most probably it was their mother. So I'd like you to take these two boys with you to Paris."

Sure enough, the captain took the two boys to

Paris. They found themselves at the same hotel as their mother, but they didn't recognize each other. They stayed at the hotel, had plenty of money. They started reading the newspaper and saw that the Pope was looking for two servants, one to get his mail and the other to give charity to the poor.

In Paris, their mother lived off charity. She was very poor, almost nothing on her body. Every day she would ask the Pope's servant, her son, for charity. They didn't know each other. One day, there was a guy who said to the Pope's servant, "Give more to that woman. I feel so for her, she looks so pitiful. I don't think she's been like this all her life."

Right away, another woman asked, "Why are you giving more to her than the others?"

"You—if you're not happy with what I'm giving you, you stay home tomorrow."

One day, Jean and Henri, who were two war officers, stopped where the charity was being handed out to the poor. They were all united there but didn't know each other. Jean didn't know that Henri was married to his daughter. Henri thought his wife was dead because his mother had told him that she'd been exiled in the forest. Beautiful Helen did not recognize her children and they didn't recognize their mother. When they were all together, they said to Jean, "You're the oldest here"—he was Beautiful Helen's father—"tell us some stories."

"I have one that I could tell you," Jean said, "but it's almost too terrible."

"Perhaps it's the best one," they said.

"Well, I believe I had the most beautiful wife in the world. She's dead. We had a daughter who was about sixteen or seventeen years old. I wanted to marry her because she was the picture of her mother. I wasn't able to marry her. She left and I never heard from her since."

Seventeen years had passed since Helen had left. Henri, who had been married to Beautiful Helen, after listening to this story, got up and went over to shake Jean's hand. He said, "You are my father-in-law. It's me that married your Beautiful Helen. The story you just told us, she told me that story herself."

Well, they found themselves all there, the whole family: Jean, The Beautiful Helen, their two children and their father Henri. Jean and Henri didn't recognize Beautiful Helen or the children. She was poor, thin and not dressed very well. She also didn't know that these two boys were her sons. She recognized her husband and her father. She didn't let on who she was for fear that they would kill her. She still thought that her husband had ordered her to be killed.

She became very tired of living this way. Two or three days later, she met up with them again on the street. She fell down to her knees in front of them and said, "Papa, Henri my husband, I'm dying of hunger. If you want to kill me, kill me right here."

Henri pushed her aside and said, "You want

150

me to think you're my wife but you're not my wife."

"Henri," she said, "if I tell you all the stories about when we met, when we were together before you went to war, will you believe I'm your wife?"

"Ah!" he said, "yes."

"Do you remember I had a birthmark of a star on my left shoulder?"

Henri answered, "Yes."

She pulled her dress down over her shoulder. The star was there.

"Ah!" he said, "I see that you're my wife, but where are our two children?"

"I don't know where they are," she replied.

Well, they went to find the Pope, in order to thank him. Henri had found his wife and Jean his daughter. Jean asked a thousand pardons of his daughter for the suffering he caused her. Henri and his wife were very worried about their children. The Pope said, "Your two children are still living. You'll find them later on."

After Mass, the Pope invited them to breakfast at the glebe house. Once there, Henri said, "I'm happy to have found my wife, but I will be even happier when I've found my two children."

The Pope said, "Look to your left, there's one; look to your right, there's the other."

Sure enough, they were both there. They flung themselves on their father and mother and hugged them.

One of the two boys had that leather bag in which was his mother's cut-off hand. The Pope took

Beautiful Helen's hand that had been cut off. It was just as beautiful as when it was cut off, as it had been embalmed to last for forty years. He placed the hand at the end of Beautiful Helen's arm. He pushed on it. The hand and the arm joined together and she used it as if it had never been cut off.

That is the story of The Beautiful Helen!

17. The Rhubarb Pie

La Tarte
à la rhubarbe

This funny tale[1] is well known in Acadia and throughout French Canada. It belongs to the cycle 1675-1724—stories of the stupid man. This man is too naive to respond to a woman's advances.

The Rhubarb Pie

THE RHUBARB PIE is a story about a girl who was seeing two guys. One guy was rich, the other was poor. She loved the poor one the most. She said to him, "If you left for two years, worked hard and saved your money, I'd prefer to marry you and not the rich guy."

"Ah well," he said, "I'm going to do it!"

She said, "Try to send me a letter every month. If you forget to send me a letter every month, I will marry the rich one." He promised he would write and then he left. But after being away for about a month, he decided not to write to her. Otherwise when he'd return home, he'd have nothing to say to her.

She waited. One month went by and no letter. Two months went by, still no letters. So she married the rich guy.

When the poor guy returned home, she met up with him on the street and announced that she was married. "Yes? You tricked me."

She said "No! I told you to write to me every month. You were two months without writing to me, so I married the rich guy. In any case, since I'm married, you're going to come visit so I can show you the beautiful house I have now."

They went to her house, and when they got there she asked him, "Do you still love rhubarb pie?"

"Ah! yes," he said, "but I've already had supper and I'm full up to here."

"Well," she said, "I'll make you one anyway."

She made him the rhubarb pie and cut it in four pieces. He ate three pieces, and she said to him, "Eat it all. I made it for you."

"I can't. I'm full."

"Ah well," she said, "if it's okay with you, I'm going to show you around the house."

She showed him her bedroom. She laid down on the bed, winked at him and said, "Whatever you ask for, I will give it to you."

"Well then," he said, "give me the other piece of rhubarb pie!"

18. The Statue of Saint Joseph

La Statue de saint Joseph

This joke[1] concerning a prudish old woman belongs to the cycle of tales 1475-1499. It indicates that an exaggerated religious devotion and prudishness can sometimes lead to embarrassing and comical situations.

The Statue of Saint Joseph

THE STORY OF THE STATUE OF SAINT JOSEPH was about a parish priest who had no statue of Saint Joseph in his church. He would have really loved to have one—that's to say, a huge man-sized statue—so he said, "Next Sunday, I will pass a collection in church to try and raise money to buy one."

It cost seventy-five dollars. He collected the seventy-five dollars the following Sunday, and he sent the money to the company so that they could send him a statue of Saint Joseph. When the statue arrived, he placed it in front of the altar for the week. He blessed it, leaving it in front of the altar. Then he called everyone in the parish to come and say the rosary at the foot of the statue. He said, "This is really nice, it's going well." But he didn't know what was to come.

155

There was an old woman who was simple-minded. She was religious but simple. She went to say the rosary, kneeling very close to the statue. You've all seen old women who sway while saying the rosary; well, she swayed. Every time she swayed, the statue rocked as well. She thought it was Saint Joseph who was giving her his benediction, in the aisle in front of the altar. She somehow ended up with the statue on top of her, and after a struggle she moved the statue and got away. She ran towards the glebe house and the priest came to greet her and said, "What's wrong with you?"

She replied, "What's wrong with me? That's not the statue of Saint Joseph that you've ordered and placed in the church. It's a lecherous guy. He threw himself on top of me right in front of the altar, and I had a hard time getting rid of him!"

19. The Cow's Urine
L'Urine de vache

This humorous tale[1] of Type 1739, *The Parson and the Calf*, is often completed by Type 1281A, *Getting Rid of the Man-eating Calf*. It is widely known all over Europe and in the Eastern countries. This is the only version collected in Acadia.

As we were unable to find, in spite of our research, the person who collected this tale to obtain authorization to have it published, we share with you a summary of the story.

The Cow's Urine

TWO BROTHERS LEAVE THE HOUSE on foot to go to America. On the way, one of them gets sick. The other goes to see the doctor with a bottle of his brother's urine, to get it analyzed. He has nothing with which to cap the bottle. While climbing over a fence, he spills the bottle and replaces it with the urine of a cow. While analyzing the urine, the doctor is aware of some trickery and declares that the sick brother is going to have a calf, and gives him pills for his pain. The sick brother believes the doctor. In short, this is a story of the great fools.

After they separate, the one that was sick discovers a dead body in a ditch, and cuts the legs off so he can have his boots. A woman puts him up for the night. And it just so happens that she has a cow that's expecting a calf.

During the night, the cow calves, and they carry the calf next to the stove where the sick brother is sleeping. He wakes up and notices the calf, and thinks he delivered the calf while he was sleeping. He takes flight, leaving the (dead man's) leg behind. When the woman discovers the leg and no young man, she comes to the conclusion that the cow ate him. When he meets up with his brother later on, he relates how well he's feeling since he delivered the calf.

20. The Lover
L'Amoureux

This short humorous tale was collected by Arthur LeBlanc[1] from Marcellin Haché (75 years old) in 1954. This does not appear in the Aarne-Thompson index. Here is the summary.

The Lover

THIS YOUNG MAN invites a young girl to go for a stroll on horseback on his old horse. Along the way, he often asks for permission to hug her. She refuses. When they arrive in a clearing, they get down from the horse and sit in the grass. The old horse is so tired that he lies down and stretches out. He's had it.

The young man once again asks the girl for a hug.

She asks the young man, "What will it do for me if you hug me?"

He answers, "Your eyes will sparkle and you will jump up in the air."

She then said, "Well, if that's the case, hug your old horse so that we can go home!"

Loubie Chiasson

Tales from Loubie Chiasson

LOUBIE CHIASSON was not recognized as a storyteller. This was doubtless because he had a limited repertoire. Nevertheless, he was very good at telling stories. Along with his sister, Mrs. Marie Aucoin, he was a colourful and prolific informer from Cheticamp, sought out by folklorists and reporters from Radio-Canada in pursuit of popular traditions, legends and songs.

Loubie Chiasson, son of Luc and Lucie Chiasson, was born on August 8th, 1909. He attended school scarcely more than five or six years, but he was very intelligent and gifted with a good memory. He composed a song on the work done at Cape Breton Highlands National Park. He was always interested in the history of our ancestors and their traditional songs, retaining much of this information. He possessed a rich repertoire of songs and was a good singer.

Perhaps his knowledge of tales was more than the three which we have collected from him and that we publish here. We will never know, as nobody has recorded any other tales from him, and he died on December 6th, 1985.

Mr. Chiasson was married twice; first on July 17th, 1934, to Marie-Rose Chiasson. His second marriage, on October 30th, 1962, was to Julie Poirier. He had seven children from his first marriage.

21. The Dog's Remembrance

La Reconnaissance du chien

This tale[1] is compared to Type 101: *The Old Dog as Rescuer of the Child (Sheep)*. Especially widespread in the Eastern countries, this Type is also found in a few European countries and in Japan. This tale is the only version recorded in Acadia.

Here, the fidelity of the dog is not presented by means of a plot conceived by his friend, the wolf, as in other versions, but instead by his keeping a voluntary distance. In both cases, a child is saved.

The Dog's Remembrance

ONCE UPON A TIME there was a farmer and his wife and they had a dog, a big beautiful dog. They were very poor, and one day the man said to his wife, "I believe we might have to kill our dog. Now that we're getting poorer, I'm not sure that we can afford to keep him."

It happened that the dog overheard this. He came to the table and ate; when he was done, he went to the door and they let him out. They didn't see the dog again—he didn't return because he overheard that they were going to kill him.

Well, two or three years later, times were better. One day the farmer said to his son, "We have to go into town to sell some livestock."

Sure enough, they left, him and his son. They went to the city. They sold their livestock and while they were getting paid, there was a guy watching them and saw that they had received some money. The farmer and his son didn't know this. They were on horseback and started back, but it was getting dark. On the way back, the same guy that had been watching them, stopped them.

They didn't recognize him, and he said to them, "At a certain place, there's a road, and you will not be able to pass because the bridge is destroyed. Take this other road and although it might take a bit longer, you'll be all right and you'll be able to pass. "

So be it. They went that way but instead of having them take the right road, he had them take the wrong one. When they arrived at a certain place, it was getting really late and, actually, it was there that the bridge was destroyed. They were very puzzled. There was a house not too far away with some light. The man said to his son, "Well, we will not be able to make it tonight. By the time we turn around and return home it'll be too late. We're going to go to that house over there."

They went to the house, knocked on the door. A man and a woman opened the door. The farmer and the boy told them what happened and asked if they could stay the night. "Well," the man answered, "I think that's okay."

Supper was prepared. While they were having supper, there was a big dog that was watching them. He was near the table and the boy was a bit scared but they didn't make a big deal of it. When they were ready for bed, the father and son entered the bedroom and so did the dog. The man of the house locked the door behind them. Then they knew something was up. The man and woman were thieves. They were accomplices to the guy who had sent them on this road. So then it was quite dark in the room; they went toward the bed to lay down but the dog went there and started growling. He wanted to stop them. They were very scared. They realized the mess they were in. What were they going to do now? They were like this for quite a while. Then the dog approached the little boy and wagged its tail. All of a sudden, he said to his father, "Do you remember the dog we used to have? Well, he really looks like him."

As soon as this was said, I guess the dog understood; that is to say, the dog recognized them. He didn't eat them because he was so happy to see them. He jumped on them and the father said, "I believe this is our dog. If it's our dog, we'll be fine. He may save us."

After a while, the dog went in a small closet and started scratching on the door. The son said to his father, "I think I'd better open that to see what's inside."

He opened the door only to find a small crowbar, a small bar of iron. The dog took this in his mouth. He was on the floor struggling to open an iron ring. So the little boy said, "I have to open this."

He opened it and underneath found some dead bodies. The thieves would make the people enter, and had trained the dog to kill. The dog would kill them and then the thieves would check them over for money.

"Ah!" his father said, "close that, close that, for the love of God!"

They kept on waiting. The next morning (they spent the night there), the same guy who had told them to take the other road came over. He asked the man and woman if two guys had come this way.

"Ah yes," the man said, "and chances are that the dog has killed them. We'll go see later on."

They overheard this and they thought, "Well, we're in some fix. The dog didn't kill us but the others might kill us now."

But no. "Ah," the thief said, "smoke your pipe. We'll go see after. There's no rush."

After they finished smoking, they went to open the door. As they opened the door, the dog jumped for the thief's throat and choked him; the others—the man and woman of the house—took off. When they were alone in the house, the dog went to a closet and scratched on the door. They went to see and found a package of money. They took the money and the father said to the dog, "You can come home with us. We can become poor again, but you will always stay with us."

So off they went home together, very happy!

166

22. The Two Fools

Les Deux Innocents

This tale[1] belongs to Type 1685: *The Foolish Bridegroom*, of the cycle of the stupid hero (Aarne-Thompson, 1675-1724) and to Type 1313: *The Man who Thought Himself Dead*, of the cycle of the story of the fool (Aarne-Thompson, 1200-1349). These joking tales are generally found in Europe and came to America during the colonial period.

Here, the difference of these Tale-Types is that there's two stupid heroes instead of one, brothers who are old bachelors. They follow their mother's advice literally—to say "good night" to the girls, to tease them by throwing little pieces of wood—but they don't understand what she means. In spite of everything, they end up marrying the girls. Eventually, the girls look for ways to get rid of them.

The Two Fools

ONE TIME, THERE WERE TWO BACHELORS who weren't very clever. They were hard workers and they lived with their mother with no talk of getting married. They were almost too simple to get married. Meanwhile their mother thought about the two girls who lived in the house nearby. She said to her sons, "You should really try to get married and do like everyone else. Maybe if you went to see the girls over there, maybe you'd have a chance to have them."

167

They said to their mother, "But we don't know how to go about it."

She replied, "Just go over, enter, then say, 'Good night'—and after that, well...."

One day one of the sons said to the other, "Tonight we're going to go over. We're going to go see them."

It came to be. So off they went. They went to the house, opened the door and said, "Good night," closed the door and returned home.

Their mother asked them, "Did you stay and visit?"

"No."

"What did you do?"

"We went over to say good night and then came home."

But the mother said, "That's not how you should do it. You have to go in, talk with them and during the evening, you can throw little twigs of wood at the girls to tease them, you know, little pieces of wood.[2] That's what you should do to get their attention."

The next day, the sons were ploughing. Simple as they were, it took both of them to do the ploughing. One of the sons said to the other, "You do the ploughing by yourself, I'm going to go cut pieces of wood."

So he left his brother there, took his saw and went to cut pieces of wood, just like firewood for the stove, a good size. He made two loads, then tied them up properly with rope and stacked them.

When night came he told his brother, "We're going to go well prepared tonight."

They washed up, got ready and took off, each with a load of wood on their backs. They went to the girls' house and entered. They sat down, placing their load of wood on the floor beside them. The girls didn't know what this was all about, but all of a sudden one of the guys winked at the other. They untied their package and started throwing the wood at the girls. When they were all finished, they were satisfied. They announced, "We're going to go home now." They left.

Their mother asked, "Did you talk this evening?"

"Ah!" they replied, "we had so much fun. We nearly killed them!" They explained what they had done.

"But," she said, "that's not the way to do this. You nearly killed them!"

"Yes, we sure laughed."

Well, all right. I don't know how it was accomplished, but they got married. They married those two girls. The two brothers had money but they were very simple. After they were married, the girls started talking about ways of getting rid of their husbands. They were bored. They had their husbands' money. One day one of the wives told her husband, "You're going to work at a certain place, and I'll bring you your lunch."

Ah! that's good. They were always game to do anything their wives asked for.

169

She left with his lunch and when she arrived, she said, "Where are you? You're not here. I've been searching a long time for you and I don't see you. Where are you?"

"Well," he said, "I don't know. I guess I'm lost."

"You're surely lost!"

"Well," he replied, "if I'm lost I need to find myself. So I'm going to go search for myself."

He couldn't find himself.

The two brothers really looked alike. While the one wife had brought lunch to her husband, the other wife had played a trick on her husband. She had made him believe that he was actually dead. She said to him, "You're dead now."

So he played dead. She put him in a coffin because she wanted to bury him, wanted to be rid of him. The other brother who was still alive believed he was lost, saw the coffin and said to himself, "Maybe it's me in that box." He figured he should take a look. So he went to see, and recognized himself.... He started roaring with laughter. He was happy. He had found himself. The brother in the coffin asked, "What are you laughing about?"

"Well," he said, "I was looking for myself and I have found myself."

"Well," the other brother said, "you're right. If I wasn't dead, I'd laugh too!"

And that's all!

23. The Fur Hat Merchant

Le Marchand de chapeaux de poils

This joking tale[1] of Type 1536B, *The Three Hunch-back Brothers Drowned*, is scattered in Europe, in the Eastern countries, in several Asian countries and even in China. Usually, as indicated in the title found in Aarne-Thompson's catalogue, the victims are three hunchbacks.

This is a story about a woman who is visited by three different men, at different hours, all in one evening. When her husband apparently comes home, she locks them up in a box of fur hats. When her husband "arrives," instead of being the fourth victim as is the case in several versions,[2] he becomes her accomplice in burning the victims with boiling water. In order to get rid of the men, she asks an idiot to bury them one by one, pretending over and over again that it's the same person who just doesn't want to die. The idiot, by doing what he thinks is right, ends up killing and burying the caretaker of the cemetery.

The Fur Hat Merchant

ONCE THERE WAS A MAN who made fur hats and he'd sell them in the city. One day he had gone to the city and his wife was home alone. I'm not sure why, but I guess she went into the city to pick up something she needed. On her way, she met up with a carpenter who was working on a building. He asked her, "Are you going to be alone at home tonight?"

"Ah, yes," she said. "Why?"

He answered, "Well, couldn't I go visit for a while? I'll pay you, I'll give you a good price."

She replied, "Sure! Come and visit me while my husband is away. He's gone to the city and he's not coming home tonight."

"Oh!" he said, "I'll give you one hundred dollars!"

"Fine, good, come on. You'll come over at seven o'clock."

He went home quite content. She continued on, and after a short distance she met up with another man. He asked for the same thing, to go visit her for a while that evening. She answered, "Yes. If you can give me one hundred dollars, you can come over. You can come at nine o'clock. I'll be free then as my husband won't be home until late, after midnight."

"Good!" she thought. "This really suits me. I am going to make some money." She continued on, and again after a short distance she met up with a third man who wanted the same thing. He wanted to spend some time with her that evening. "Well," she said, "I guess so, but you'll have to come over late. I have some work to do and I won't be free until ten o'clock. After that it'll be all right!"

So be it. She went home. Not long after, her husband arrived. She told him, "I want you to hide somewhere. I'm going to make some money tonight. I will not tell you what I've done, just leave me be. Hide and let me do this and don't say anything. Don't come out."

So around seven o'clock, the first man she had talked to arrived. He was all dressed up, handed her the one hundred dollars, and they chatted away. They chatted while she worked. She ironed the clothing and chatted away, making the time go by faster. All of a sudden, they heard a knock on the door. He was very surprised and asked, "Who could that be?"

"Well," she said, "I don't know. It must be my husband back from the city. Something must have happened."

"Well," he asked, "where are you going to put me?"

She replied, "There's a box behind the stove. Hide inside the box and I'll put a cover over it. He won't find you."

So that's what he did. He hid inside the box and she put a cover over it. But it wasn't her husband that was arriving, it was the second man. The man hiding in the box didn't say a word, he just stayed hidden. She did the same thing with the second man—he was very nice—she took his money and chatted away. After a little while, Bang! Bang! Bang! on the door again. Again, the same carry-on.

He asked, "What is that?"

"Something must have happened that my husband had to come home."

"Well," he said, "where are you going to put me?"

"You can hide in that box."

Sure enough, she hid the second man in the box on top of the other man who was already hiding—not a word—closed the cover. That made two of them. The third man came in, gave his money, and they talked and talked. Meanwhile her husband who was hiding all this time figured this time he was really going to show up. So he went out and knocked on the door.

The third man asked, "Who could that be? Who's knocking at the door?"

"Well, it must be my husband, something must have happened and he had to come home."

"Where are you going to put me?"

"Well," she replied, "in that box over there."

So sure enough, she hid the third man on top of the other two men in the box, and firmly closed the cover. Her husband came in. "My God," he said, "hurry up and boil some water. I just got an order for a lot of hats. The order has to be done by tomorrow or the day after. I have to heat up the fur to make my hats."

She boiled some water and her husband went over to the box with the hidden men; the cover of the box was full of holes. He poured the hot boiling water into the holes. This burned the men but they didn't say one word, not one measly word. When he

174

was finished, his wife said, "Well, you sure did it this time. We could be caught. I had made it quite clear for you to stay hidden. Well anyway, I have the solution."

At the time, there was this man who was very simple-minded. He used to walk on the road at night and always stopped in at the last house that was lit up. If he saw some light coming from the house, he'd go over to visit. So they waited until they heard him coming, whistling away. He used to whistle all the time. When she heard him coming, she took one of the men out of the box and sat him in a chair. She told her husband to hide. When the simple man arrived, he went up to the man in the chair and asked, "Who's this idiot, doesn't he talk?"

"Well, he came over to visit and dropped dead in his chair. I don't know what to do about it. I don't suppose you could get rid of him for us?"

"Yes," he said. "If you give me a shot of whisky and a piece of bread, I'll go bury him for you."

"Sure," she said, "and come back here after and I'll give you another shot of whisky."

Sure enough, he took a good drink of whisky and then took off, carrying the dead body on his back. He arrived at the cemetery, dug a grave, gave him an overall beating before burying him. While he was doing this, the woman had taken another man out of the box and sat him in the same chair. When the simple man returned to the house, she said to him, "Look, he must have escaped, you didn't bury him."

He examined the dead body and replied, "Well, if you want to give me another shot of whisky, I'll go bury him, and I guarantee you that he won't get away this time!"

So off he went. This made two bodies. He arrived at the cemetery and again beat the body twice as much to make sure he didn't escape. Then he dug a grave and buried him. When he returned to the house, the woman had put the third body in the chair. She said, "He escaped again. You were barely out the door and he was back here."

The simple man became enraged. "Just give me another drink of whisky, and this time I guarantee you he won't return."

So he left with the body over his back, went and dug another hole and then he beat him up. Meanwhile, there was someone who would watch the cemetery. He saw all this and was very curious as to what was going on. He thought it was very odd for someone to haul bodies in this manner. He walked closer and closer to the graves. The simple man saw him and thought this was the dead body trying to escape again. He took off after him. When they got to a fence, he stabbed the watchman in the back with his pick and killed him. He then buried him and returned to the house.

"Ah!" the woman said, "he didn't escape this time. You did a good job!"

"But he almost got away. I ran after him and caught him right at the fence. I almost had to make another trip. Now, I'm satisfied."

She said, "What do you want now?"

"Well," he replied, "give me a good drink of whisky and then I'll be on my way. I'm going home satisfied. I was determined to bury him even if I had to run after him until morning!"

That's all!

Notes

Preface

1. Anselme Chiasson and Daniel Boudreau, Capuchin Fathers, *Chansons d'Acadie*. 7 vols. La Réparation, Pointe-aux-Trembles (Montreal), 1942, 1945, 1948; Editions des Aboiteaux, Moncton, 1972, 1979; Cheticamp, Les Trois Pignons, 1983, 1985. Daniel Boudreau, *Chansons d'acadie*, vols. 8-11, Cheticamp, no date, 1986, no date, 1987, 1993.
2. Anselme Chiasson, *Chéticamp, histoire et traditions acadiennes*, Editions des Aboiteaux, Moncton, 1962. *Cheticamp, History and Acadian Traditions*, translation by Jean Doris LeBlanc, Breakwater Editions, St. John's, 1986, 331 pages.

Introduction

1. *Chéticamp, op. cit.*, p. 268.
2. Gérald E. Aucoin, *L'oiseau de la vérité et autres contes des pêcheurs acadiens de l'île du Cap-Breton*, Editions Quinze, Mémoires d'homme, Montreal, and The Museum of Man, Ottawa, 1980, 225 pages.
3. Letter, April 15th, 1994.

1. The Black Dog

1. Collection of Fr. Anselme Chiasson, Centre d'études acadiennes, Université de Moncton, tape 258. Told August 15, 1957, by Marcellin Haché (age 78) of Cheticamp, Nova Scotia. This story was published in *Cape Breton's Magazine*, No. 27, December 1980, pp. 28-31.

179

2. In the present work, the classification of the stories is made with the help of *The Types of the Folktale*, by Antti Aarne and Stith Thompson, Academy of Sciences of Finland, Helsinki, 1961, 588 pages, FF Communications, No. 184.

3. Aarne-Thompson, *op. cit.*, p. 244-245.

4. Paul Delarue and Marie-Louise Tenèze, *Le Conte populaire français*, vol. II, Maisonneuve et Larose, Paris, 1964, p. 726.

2. The Fountain of Youth

1. Collection of Fr. Anselme Chiasson, Centre d'études acadiennes, Université de Moncton, tape 259. Told August 15, 1957, by Marcellin Haché (age 78) of Cheticamp, N.S. This story was published in *Cape Breton's Magazine*, No. 64, August 1993, pp. 59-66.

2. According to Delarue and Tenèze, *op. cit.*, p. 358.

3. Aarne-Thompson, *op. cit.*, pp. 195-197.

4. Delarue and Tenèze, *op. cit.*, pp. 720-721. In 1954, researching for a master's thesis entitled "La Chandeleur chez les Acadiens de l'île du Cap-Breton" (Université Laval, Quebec), Arthur Le-Blanc collected this story from this same storyteller in a very abridged and incomplete version (pp. 77-81). The conclusion is the same.

3. The Little Pig

1. Collection of Fr. Anselme Chiasson, Centre d'études acadiennes, Université de Moncton, tape 269. Told August 22, 1957, by Marcellin Haché (age 78) of Cheticamp, N.S.

2. Clément Legaré, *Pierre la fève et autres contes de la Mauricie*, Ed. Quinze, Montréal, 1982, p. 63.

3. Aarne-Thompson, *op. cit.*, p. 448.

4. Clément Legaré, *op. cit.*

5. Ronald Labelle *et al.*, *Inventaire des sources en folklore acadien*, CEA, Université de Moncton, Moncton, 1984, p. 27.

4. The Mother's Arms

1. Collection of Fr. Anselme Chiasson, Centre d'études acadiennes, Université de Moncton, tape 265. Told August 21, 1957, by Marcellin Haché (age 78) of Cheticamp, N.S. Hélène Bernier, in her work, *La Fille aux mains coupées*, tale-type 706 (PUL, Quebec, 1971, p. 67), offers an analysis of this version.

2. Hélène Bernier, *op. cit.*, p. 4-5.

3. *Ibid.*, p. 5-6.

4. *Ibid.*, p. 4.

5. *Ibid.*, p. 8-26.

6. *Ibid.*, p. 27.

7. Collection of Fr. Anselme Chiasson, Archives de folklore de l'Université Laval, Quebec, tape 272.

8. Collection of Luc Lacourcière, Archives de folklore de l'Université Laval, Quebec, tape 3963.

5. The Stingiest King in the World

1. Collection of Fr. Anselme Chiasson, Centre d'études acadiennes, Université de Moncton, tape 272. Told August 8, 1957, by Marcellin Haché (age 78) of Cheticamp, N.S.

2. Aarne-Thompson, *op. cit.*, pp. 446-447.

3. Ronald Labelle, *op. cit.*, p. 27.

6. The Three Rabbits

1. Collection of Fr. Anselme Chiasson, Centre d'études acadiennes, Université de Moncton, tape 262. Told August 15, 1957, by Marcellin Haché (age 78) of Cheticamp, N.S.
2. Clément Legaré, *La Bête à sept têtes et autres contes de la Mauricie*, Montreal, Éd. Quinze, 1980, p. 105.
3. Delarue and Tenèze, *op. cit.*, pp. 722-723.

7. The Three Burned Children

1. Aarne-Thompson, *op. cit.*, p. 118.
2. Collection of Fr. Anselme Chiasson, Centre d'études acadiennes, Université de Moncton, tape 270. Told August 21, 1957, by Marcellin Haché (age 78) of Cheticamp, N.S. This story was published in *Cape Breton's Magazine*, No. 55, August 1990, pp. 66-68.
3. Gérald E. Aucoin, *op cit.*, pp. 71-80.
4. Méderic Roach, a neighbour.

8. One Thousand Dollars for a Dozen Eggs

1. Collection of Fr. Anselme Chiasson, Centre d'études acadiennes, Université de Moncton, tape 274. Told August 21, 1957, by Marcellin Haché (age 78) of Cheticamp, N.S.
2. Aarne-Thompson, *op. cit.*, pp. 277-278.

9. The Shrewd Thief

1. Collection of Fr. Anselme Chiasson, Centre

d'études acadiennes, Université de Moncton, tape 264. Told August 15, 1957, by Marcellin Haché (age 78) of Cheticamp, N.S. This story was published in *Cape Breton's Magazine*, No. 25, June 1979, pp. 29-34. Gérald E. Aucoin, in his collection of stories *L'Oiseau de la vérité, op. cit.*, pp. 151-164, published a version of this tale collected in 1951 from the same storyteller.

2. Aarne-Thompson, *op. cit.*, p. 432.

3. Ronald Labelle, *op. cit.*, p. 27, counts thirteen Acadian versions.

10. The Most Beautiful Girl in the World

1. Collection of Fr. Anselme Chiasson, Centre d'études acadiennes, Université de Moncton, tape 268. Told August 15, 1957, by Marcellin Haché (age 78) of Cheticamp, N.S.

2. Delarue and Tenèze, *op. cit.*, p. 718.

3. Gérald E. Aucoin, *op. cit.*, pp. 99-112.

11. The Fourteen Thieves

1. Collection of Fr. Anselme Chiasson, Centre d'études acadiennes, Université de Moncton, tape 267. Told August 15, 1957, by Marcellin Haché (age 78) of Cheticamp, N.S.

2. When he came to the end of the story, when the fourteenth thief lost his head, the storyteller, Marcellin Haché, told us that the girl who had cut off the heads of the thirteen thieves was the wife of the fourteenth thief. That happened like a hair in the soup, because there was nothing said about the marriage before that. In reality, in Cheticamp,

183

they know in this story that the leader of the fourteen thieves passes himself off as an honest man to the father of the young girl. She agrees to marry him at the request of her father, to whom she has promised to never say no. But Mr. Haché forgot, and omitted all that part of the story.

12. The Boy Who Was Good Company

1. Collection of Fr. Anselme Chiasson, Centre d'études acadiennes, Université de Moncton, tape 271. Told August 21, 1957, by Marcellin Haché (age 78) of Cheticamp, N.S. This story was published in *Cape Breton's Magazine*, No. 61, August 1992, pp. 31-40. Arthur LeBlanc, *op. cit.*, pp. 83-89, collected a version of the same story from Mr. Haché in 1954.
2. Aarne-Thompson, *op. cit.*, p. 173.
3. The version of Jean Z. Deveau in *L'Oiseau de la vérité*, *op. cit.*, pp. 113-124, offers a few differences. The king is replaced by a rich merchant, the young boy becomes a poor neighbour and the trickery that the young man uses to marry the girl is not the same. Finally, instead of leaving, the young man builds a house next door to that of his parents.

13. The Seven-Headed Beast

1. Gérald E. Aucoin, *op. cit.*, p. 51.
2. Collection of Fr. Anselme Chiasson, Centre d'études acadiennes, Université de Moncton, tape 260. Told August 8, 1957, by Marcellin Haché (age 78) of Cheticamp, N.S.

14. The Princess with Golden Hair

1. Collection of Fr. Anselme Chiasson, Centre

d'études acadiennes, Université de Moncton, tape 266. Told August 15, 1957, by Marcellin Haché (age 78) of Cheticamp, N.S.

2. Gérald E. Aucoin, *op. cit.*, pp. 179-194.

15. The Bird of Truth

1. Collection of Fr. Anselme Chiasson, Centre d'études acadiennes, Université de Moncton, tape 263. Told August 15, 1957, by Marcellin Haché (age 78) of Cheticamp, N.S.

2. Aarne-Thompson, *op. cit.*, pp. 92-93.

3. Gérald E. Aucoin, *op. cit.*, pp. 165-178.

4. From this point on, the ending of this story, as I collected it from Marcellin Haché, is not clear. By using the version that I collected, along with the one—scarcely any clearer—collected from the same storyteller and published by Gérald E. Aucoin, and by adding the memory I have of hearing this story during my adolescence, I present here an ending that is clearer and more logical.

16. The Beautiful Helen

1. Collection of Luc Lacourcière, No. 3963, Archives de folklore of the Université Laval, Quebec. Told in August 1960 by Marcellin Haché (age 81) from Cheticamp, N.S. Published here with the authorization of the Archives de folklore, given by Mrs. Carole Saulnier, co-ordinator of the management program of the archives.

17. The Rhubarb Pie

1. Collection of Fr. Anselme Chiasson, Centre d'études acadiennes, Université de Moncton, tape

261. Told August 21, 1957, by Marcellin Haché (age 78) of Cheticamp, N.S.

18. The Statue of Saint Joseph

1. Collection of Fr. Anselme Chiasson, Centre d'études acadiennes, Université de Moncton, tape 273. Told August 21, 1957, by Marcellin Haché (age 78) of Cheticamp, N.S.

19. The Cow's Urine

1. Collection of Gérald Aucoin, Centre d'études acadiennes, Université de Moncton, tape 2. Told in 1972 by Marcellin Haché (age 93) of Cheticamp, N.S. This Gérald Aucoin, also from Cape Breton, is not the one who published *L'Oiseau de la vérité*.

20. The Lover

1. This tale is found in a master's thesis: *La Chandeleur chez les Acadiens du Cap-Breton*, Université Laval, Quebec, 1954, pp. 81-82, by Arthur LeBlanc, also from Cape Breton.

21. The Dog's Remembrance

1. Collection of Fr. Anselme Chiasson, Centre d'études acadiennes, Université de Moncton, tape 307. Told in September 1958 by Loubie Chiasson (age 49) of Cheticamp, N.S.

22. The Two Fools

1. Collection of Fr. Anselme Chiasson, Centre d'études acadiennes, Université de Moncton, tape 306. Told in September 1958 by Loubie Chiasson (age 49) of Cheticamp, N.S. This story was published in *Cape Breton's Magazine*, No. 23, August

1979, pp. 1 and 37-38.

2. It was an old custom to throw a match or a little twig to invite the girl to go sit to one side with the boy.

23. The Fur Hat Merchant

1. Collection of Fr. Anselme Chiasson, Centre d'études acadiennes, Université de Moncton, tape 305. Told in September 1958 by Loubie Chiasson (age 49) of Cheticamp, N.S.

2. See Marius Barbeau, *Veillées du bon vieux temps à la Bibliothèque Saint-Sulpice à Montréal, les 18 mars et 24 avril 1919*, under the auspices of La Sociéte historique de Montréal and La Société de folklore d'Amérique, section de Québec (American Folklore Society), Montreal, G. Ducharme, editor, 1920, pp. 70-72.

Index of Types
According to Aarne-Thompson

Other books by Anselme Chiasson include:

Chéticamp, histoire et traditions acadiennes, Moncton, Editions des Aboiteaux, 1972 (1962, 1961).

Légendes des îles de la Madeleine, Moncton, Editions d'Acadie, 1976.

Chéticamp, History and Acadian Traditions, Jean Doris LeBlanc (trans.), Breakwater Editions, 1986.

Le Diable Frigolet et 24 autres contes des îles de la Madeleine, Moncton, Editions d'Acadie, 1991.

L'Histoire de tapis "hookés" de Chéticamp et de leurs artisans, Yarmouth, Editions Lescarbot, 1985, illus., coll. Mme. Annie-Rose Deveau.

The History of Chéticamp Hook Rugs and their Artisans, Marcel LeBlanc (trans.), Yarmouth, Editions Lescarbot, 1988.

Le Nain Jaune et 17 autres contes des îles de la Madeleine, Moncton, Editions d'Acadie, 1995.

continued on next page . . .